Searchi...

Searching For Sex

Emma Allan

X
LIBRIS

An X *Libris* Book

First published in Great Britain in 1998
by X Libris
This edition published in 1999

Copyright © Emma Allan 1998

The moral right of the author has been asserted.

A CIP catalogue record for this book
is available from the British Library.

ISBN 0 7515 2954 0

Photoset in North Wales by
Derek Doyle & Associates, Mold, Clwyd
Printed and bound in Great Britain by
Clays Ltd, St Ives plc

X Libris
A Division of
Little, Brown and Company (UK)
Brettenham House
Lancaster Place
London WC2E 7EN

Searching For Sex

Prologue

THE FORD ESCORT pulled out of the driveway of their house. She ducked below the level of the dashboard so he wouldn't see her. It turned left at the roundabout a hundred yards down the road. She started her car and gave chase, staying well behind, not wanting him to spot her if he glanced in his rear-view mirror.

He wouldn't recognise the car. She'd hired it an hour ago. As far as he was concerned, she was in Manchester until Friday – that's what she'd told him. He had no reason to be suspicious. There had been many nights away from home; her job demanded it. And that was the trouble. She had given him too much opportunity.

She knew he was having an affair. He had been having one for the last four months, she was sure of it. All the signs were there. He was never at home when she rang from which ever ghastly provincial hotel she was staying in. He never wanted to make love to her when she got home. Then there were the phone calls, a caller who refused to speak if she answered the phone.

Kate Hailstone was not a fool. She could put two and two together. The fact that she had found a used condom packet in the pocket of his jacket yesterday afternoon just served to confirm everything she'd suspected.

Her first emotion, if she were truthful with herself, was relief. Her marriage to Sean had not been going well even before his affair. She supposed she should have just faced him with it there and then, and asked for a divorce, but curiosity got the better of her. She wanted to know who he was seeing. She was interested to know whose charms he rated higher than her own. She wondered if it might even be Mandy Summers, one of their neighbours, whose long legs and blonde hair had always attracted her husband, and whose flirtatious manner with him had indicated the attraction might well be mutual.

So she had carefully rearranged her schedule, picked up the hire car at the end of her working day and driven straight to her house, parking just around the corner where she could see the entrance to their driveway. She watched Sean arrive home and, sure enough, watched him emerge thirty minutes later.

The Ford Escort was white and easy to follow. It swung onto the dual carriageway, going south, and Kate tucked her Mondeo in behind it. The pursuit did not last long. After three or four miles, the Escort indicated left and turned onto a small country lane. After half a mile or so, Kate saw a large, modern and totally anonymous hotel set in an acre of concrete car park, landscaped with plane trees growing in large circular concrete planters.

Pulling over to the side of the road, she waited and watched Sean get out of the car and walk through the large glass doors that fronted the main entrance, carrying a small case. As soon as he had gone inside she drove into the car park and parked her car. She waited, estimating how long it would take to register, then be taken to his room. Would his lover already be here, recumbent on the inevitable double bed, her slender body swathed in a black satin négligé? Sean had always had a penchant for high heels. Would his lover have been briefed to provide this delight?

She gave him thirty minutes, then got out of the car, feeling surprisingly calm. Up until now she supposed that all her suspicions, even the evidence of the used condom packet, might be unfounded and have some other explanation. But the moment that Sean's car had turned into the hotel she knew for certain that they were not. According to him, he was going to spend a quiet night at home, working on one of his accounts. Now she knew he had lied.

The glass doors slid open automatically as she approached.

'Good evening,' she said to the receptionist behind the long, fake wood counter immediately to the left of the entrance.

'Good evening, madam,' the young man said. 'How may we help?'

'I'm meeting Mr Hailstone. Sean Hailstone.'

'Certainly, madam. Hold on a minute.' The man tapped the computer terminal at his side. 'He's in room 120. I'll call him for you.' He picked up the phone.

'No,' Kate said quickly. 'No. Don't do that . . . I . . . The truth is, it's a surprise.' She smiled seductively, hoping to suggest all sorts of scenarios.

'Of course,' the man said at once. 'Just follow the corridor round to the right. It's on the ground floor.'

'Thank you.'

The young man gave her an appreciative look that suggested Sean Hailstone was a lucky man.

Kate strode off down the corridor.

Her planning had got her this far but no further. She had imagined following Sean to some rendezvous but what she would do after that she had no idea. Was she going to knock on his hotel room door and force her way in? Was she going to wait outside until the couple came out?

Room 120 was at the far end of a long corridor. She stood outside indecisively. She could hear nothing from inside.

'Can I help?' A young chambermaid had appeared from a door marked 'Staff Only'. She was pushing a trolley laden with towels and cleaning equipment.

'Oh, sorry. Forgot my key. Better go back to reception.'

'No, it's all right. Here . . .' The chambermaid took a key from her pocket, unlocked the door of room 120 and opened it.

'Thanks,' Kate said.

'No problem,' the chambermaid answered, moving away. She used the same key on the room next door and entered it, smiling at Kate as she did so.

Committed now, Kate edged through the door. She found herself in a small hallway. There was a bathroom on her right, a large open wardrobe with a line of empty hangers on the left and another door immediately in front of her which presumably led to the bedroom.

As quietly as she could she closed the exterior door. She listened. She could hear a faint moaning sound and there was no doubt that it was a moan of pleasure.

She edged towards the bedroom door; it was firmly closed. The moaning noise increased, becoming louder and longer. She supposed she should have just burst in, caught them *in flagrante delicto*, ranted at Sean and his girlfriend for a few minutes then walked out, out of the hotel and out of his life. But she didn't. Curiosity took hold of her once again.

She gripped the door handle and eased it down slowly and quietly, then pushed the door open until there was a big enough gap for her to see.

Sean was naked and kneeling on the floor by the double bed. A pair of long and slender legs were hooked over his shoulders. The legs were sheathed in sheer black hosiery – the nylon woven with Lycra to give it a glassy sheen – and taut black suspenders that pulled the jet black welts of the stockings into chevrons on creamy thighs. Red patent leather high-heeled shoes with an ankle strap – their heels the highest Kate had ever seen – were digging into Sean's back rhythmically, urging him to greater efforts while their owner whimpered, the noise she made oddly deep and husky.

The woman's face was obscured by Sean's body, but Kate could see her long black hair streaming across the dark blue counterpane of the bed – which they had clearly been in too much of a hurry to remove.

Fascinated, Kate remained absolutely still for a moment as she watched Sean's head bobbing up and down. It was ironical, she supposed, that Sean had never been keen on performing this particular service for her.

Enough is enough, she thought after a few minutes. The moans of pleasure from the woman were nearly continuous, and so baritone they were almost like a man's.

'Good evening, Sean,' she said quietly.

She expected him to be surprised. What she did not expect was to be even more astonished herself. As Sean spun around, the alarm and shock written all over his face, the figure on the bed sat up. The black suspenders were attached to an extremely tight black satin basque that was clinched down the front with red laces. The bra of the basque was not filled with quivering female breasts but semi-circular flesh-coloured plastic. The long black hair was a wig, its tresses falling around a face that, though admittedly rather feminine and fully made-up with lipstick, eye-shadow, eye-liner and blusher, definitely belonged to a man. And to confirm it there was a large erection rising from his loins, the condom that covered it glistening with Sean's saliva.

Kate had imagined that, faced with the truth of his infidelity, she would be calm and collected. She had prepared a few *bon mots*. They all deserted her. As she stared at the object of her husband's affections she felt a peculiar pulse of desire. In the black stockings his carefully shaved legs were quite as good as hers.

'Kate, look, I can explain,' Sean said, with absolutely no conviction.

'Don't bother,' she said.

She walked out of his room and out of his life. At least that bit of her plan had worked out as she'd expected.

Chapter One

'SO YOU'RE DIVORCED?'

'Yes.'

'How long ago?'

'Two years.'

'And?'

She wasn't sure what else he wanted her to say. 'I'm sorry?'

He smiled. He had a lovely smile. His lips were thin and very smooth and the philtrum deep. Her mother had always told her that's where an angel had left its fingerprint. The angel must have pressed hard in his case. 'I mean, did it leave scars, hang-ups?'

They were sitting in a small Italian restaurant in the King's Road, which had white walls and a terracotta floor. She had only known him a week. He was a barrister she'd instructed on an industrial injuries case where the insurance company were stubbornly refusing to settle. He'd asked her out to dinner after their second case conference.

Kate Hailstone looked into his dark blue eyes.

8

'Yes. It was probably more traumatic than I like to admit. I like to kid myself it didn't matter. But it was partly my fault. I got married before I realised my career was going to be the most important thing in my life.'

'The most important thing?' he queried, raising one eyebrow.

'Yes.'

'You won't get married again?'

'I might. But it's not a priority.' She looked across the table at him. Duncan Andrews was the most attractive man she had met in a long time. He was tall and slender but with broad shoulders that suggested a powerful physique. He had short brown hair and his face was handsome with a straight rather small nose and a firm jaw. But it was his eyes that had first drawn Kate. Their colour reminded her of the sea, the blue of the ocean far out from shore. 'And what about you? Are you married?'

'I was. Separated now.'

'And?' she mimicked.

'Actually, I think I could use the same reasons as you. My career came first. I'm not a homebird.'

The waiter arrived with two steaming plates of fettucine Alfredo. He refilled their glasses from the bottle of Frascati that sat in the metal ice bucket swathed in pink linen.

The pasta was delicious.

Since her divorce Kate had found it increasingly difficult to meet eligible and appealing men. The men that she came into contact with during the course of her work as a solicitor tended to be too old, too young or too married. There was a fourth category that she didn't like to admit to publicly because such things weren't supposed to matter, but the truth was that a lot of the men she met were also too unattractive. She just couldn't see herself with a fat lump of a man with a large gut, three double chins and breath that smelt of stale beer and cigarettes – which was why she was feeling increasingly more at ease with Duncan Andrews.

They talked shop as they ate. Duncan told her about the implications of the last case he'd worked on which was going to appeal and she told him about the way a rogue barrister had handled one of her cases, but her mind wasn't really on it. She kept wondering what it would be like to unbutton his white shirt and run her hand over his chest. His wrists and the back of his hands were covered in quite thick brown hair and she imagined his chest was hairy too. She'd always loved that.

They had ordered fish as a main course: grilled sea bass, a speciality of this establishment according to Duncan, whose choice it had been.

'I suppose every man you've ever been out with tells you that you're beautiful,' he said as they dissected the fish.

Kate smiled. She had never had any trouble attracting men. She had a slim body that curved in and out at all the right places and jet black hair, cut into a neat bob that was shorter at the back than at the front. Her face was rather elongated, she thought, and her nose slightly too pronounced, but her dark brown eyes were large and her cheek-bones high. Her best feature was her legs. They were long and contoured, her calves neat and her ankles pinched. She kept them that way by a rigorous exercise regime. 'If you want the truth, I haven't gone out with that many men recently.'

'I find that hard to believe.'

'Believe it. If I find a man who is even half-decent, you can bet he's married.'

'Perhaps you haven't been looking in the right places.'

'Actually, I suppose I haven't been looking at all.' That was true. Kate had been totally absorbed in her work. A year ago she had been made the youngest partner her firm had ever had and drew in billing hours that meant she could afford to move from the suburban house she'd shared with Sean to a terraced house in Kensington.

'Does that imply lack of interest?' he said.

'I get discouraged easily,' she replied.

The remains of the sea bass were taken away and they decided against dessert. They ordered espresso coffee and *vin santo*.

'I've really enjoyed myself,' Duncan said as he sipped the wine.

'So have I.' Kate looked into his eyes. She didn't want the evening to end.

'Look,' he said, 'I only live just around the corner. Why don't you come around for whatever euphemism you care to name?'

Kate laughed. At the same time she felt a sharp pulse of excitement. 'How about we skip the

11

euphemisms altogether?' she said uncharacteristically, for once allowing her instincts to override her caution.

'What a very civilised arrangement,' he said. He smiled without smugness.

'Deal.'

They finished their coffee and Duncan paid the bill with his American Express Gold card.

Outside it was a pleasant summer's night. He took her arm and they walked lazily. He lived in a flat-fronted Georgian house off Smith Street.

'Nice,' she said as he let her into the front door.

As he closed the door behind them, he grabbed her by the wrist and pulled her into his arms, covering her mouth with his and plunging his tongue between her lips. His body was muscular and hard, his strong arms wrapping themselves around her. She gasped.

'You said you didn't want euphemisms,' he said, breaking away.

'I don't,' Kate said, her heart beating like a wild bird trapped in a cage.

'Good.'

He kissed her again, harder if that were possible, crushing her against his chest. She could feel his penis swelling rapidly. She ran her hands over his back, down to his buttocks. They were small and hard, exciting her.

His mouth moved to her neck, sucking and licking and nibbling at her flesh as she threw her head back, the sinews of her throat stretched like cords of rope. She felt her sex melting, like ice-cream in hot sun, producing a sticky wetness. She realised that she actually couldn't remember the last time she'd had sex.

Duncan's hand ran over her breast, cupping it then rubbing his palm against her nipple. She felt both nipples stiffen, creating hard pebbles of sensitivity that tingled as he moved his hand from one to the other. The sensation made her gasp for a second time.

'You want it, don't you?' he whispered.

'God yes,' she muttered.

He wrapped one arm around her neck and the other around her knees, and lifted her into his arms without any apparent effort. There was a straight staircase in front of them and he climbed it without the slightest hesitation.

On the first floor landing there were three doors. He kicked one of them open and carried her inside. The bedroom was large, the double bed covered with a white silk counterpane.

Kate was so turned on she found it hard to remember to breathe.

Duncan lowered her to the bed and kissed her again, more gently this time.

'You're very strong,' she said. 'I like that.'

'And you're very beautiful, Kate.'

He stripped off his jacket and threw it on the floor. The skirt of Kate's sleeveless black dress had ridden up over her thighs and Duncan was staring at them, at her flesh sheathed in sheer champagne-coloured nylon.

'Let me get undressed,' she said, trying to sit up.

13

But Duncan had other ideas. 'No time,' he said. He leant forward to kiss her again. This time as he plunged his tongue between her lips he unbuttoned the front of her dress and forced his hand under the material until he found her bra. He slid his hand under the black lace of this garment too and closed on her right nipple; Kate moaned as he pinched it.

'God, I want you so much,' he said.

Kate never did things like this. Sex had always been a considered and calculated part of a relationship with a man. She had never allowed herself to be seduced on the first date. Judging from the extraordinary sensations she was feeling now, that had been a mistake.

Leaving her breast, his hand ran down over her belly. He pushed it up between her legs and Kate felt a huge throb of pleasure as it nudged against her sex. Almost unconsciously she opened her legs wider.

Duncan slid down the bed. As he rubbed his hand against the nylon and silk that covered her crotch his lips kissed the inside of her thigh. He worked himself around until he was kneeling between her legs. There was a seam right down the centre of her tights. Using both hands, he gripped the nylon and pulled it away from her body. She heard a ripping sound and felt the nylon giving way. Almost before she realised what he had done his fingers were pulling her black panties aside and his hot lips had descended on her labia, kissing it like a mouth.

The sensation was overwhelming. Her whole body trembled and her sex oozed a sticky nectar. She had little pubic hair between her legs but what there was had already been plastered down by her wetness. Duncan's tongue was insinuating between her labia; as he found her clitoris she moaned loudly. He flicked it to one side, then pressed it back against the underlying bone just as she felt his hand working up under her thigh, still sheathed in nylon. His fingers found the entrance to her vagina and pushed inside, one, then two, screwing up into her and again making her moan. The juices of her body had coated the cleft of her buttocks. Immediately she felt a third finger exploring the little puckered crater of her anus. Her sphincter resisted momentarily, then relaxed, allowing his finger to slip inside. He wriggled all three around, the thin membrane that separated them suddenly as sensitive as her clitoris.

She was moaning continuously now. She'd never thought of herself as a noisy lover, but then it was a long time since a man had done anything like this to her. In fact she was having trouble remembering anyone who had.

The fingers pushed deeper. As they did the tip of Duncan's tongue began to circle her clitoris with the regularity of the second hand on a watch. The whole circuit was a wonderful tour of delight but Kate soon realised that there was one particular spot that caused absolute paroxysms of pleasure. Her body was arched off the bed and each time his tongue passed the fatal spot, her body seemed to arch higher. She heard herself cry out in ecstasy too, louder and longer each time, because each touch was not an isolated event but part of a progression that she realised, in a matter of seconds, was taking her to the brink of orgasm and beyond.

Suddenly he changed tactics. He pushed his three fingers as deep as they would go, sensing that her climax was approaching rapidly, then, abandoning the circular tour, managed to concentrate his tongue on that one ultra sensitive spot, just skating back and forth over it.

Every muscle in Kate's body was rigid, her body bent like a long bow off the bed. She felt an enormous wave of feeling, so sharp it was almost painful, then a shock of pleasure that seemed to go on forever, rippling through every nerve.

Her mind just seemed to close down, wiped of everything but pure sensation. She was only vaguely aware of his fingers being pulled out of her, her body limp as a rag doll, her eyes closed, the darkness behind them pulsing purple and scarlet.

That did not last long. Instantly she felt a new set of sensations. How he had freed himself from his clothing she didn't know but suddenly Duncan's cock was nosing between her labia, its breadth spreading them apart. It nudged quite deliberately against her swollen clitoris, making her body shudder, then dived lower. He bucked his hips and plunged into the liquid centre of her sex, the lubrication she had produced making the penetration frictionless, his cock driving all the way up into her, past where his fingers had dallied, until his glans was butting against the neck of her womb and his pubic bone was grinding against hers.

He filled her completely. Perhaps it was because it had been such a long time since a man had been inside her, or perhaps he had an especially large and very hard cock, but whatever the reason Kate could not remember ever having felt her vagina filled to this extent. The feeling created such a shock of pleasure that, almost before her first orgasm had died, a second was being born, swelling up like a musical crescendo.

Her first orgasm had been sharp and centred on her clitoris. The second was totally different, an all-embracing pleasure that got stronger and more profound, gathering strength from her emotions, feeding on itself, until it had affected every nerve in her body. They all sang in unison, a vast chorus of passion that continued to resonate for a long time.

'What are you doing to me?' she managed to say after the impact had begun, finally, to die away.

'I'd have thought that was perfectly obvious,' he said, raising himself on his elbows and smiling down at her.

She glanced down between their bodies. He had managed to pull his trousers down to his knees. Her dress was rucked up around her waist and she could see the tear he had made in her tights. At the apex of her thighs she saw the thick rod of his

17

phallus half-buried in her sex, her black panties pulled over to one side.

'Let me undress,' she said.

'Not yet.' He kissed her on the mouth again, very lightly, then began moving his cock in and out of her, all the way in and almost all the way out again. It felt delicious. She dropped her head back onto the bed, the sensations too good to ignore. She felt his hand feeling for her breasts again, pushing the cups of her bra aside. Then his mouth moved onto her left breast and his teeth fastened around her nipple. He nipped the hard bud of flesh sharply. A new pleasure trembled through her body. It seemed to run directly down to her clitoris, the two connected as if an electrical circuit had just been completed. To her astonishment she felt the tell-tale signs of orgasm stirring again, her sex clenching around the bone-hard cock inside her, her clitoris pulsing wildly.

She ran her hands down over his buttocks, feeling the hard muscle as it drove him forward. That too increased her excitement.

'You'll make me come again,' she warned.

'That's what I want.'

He introduced a new tactic now. Instead of thrusting back and forth, he plunged his dick as deep as it could go and held it there, grinding its base against her clitoris. It was perfect. Perfect. She felt her body opening for him, letting him in even deeper, her feelings concentrated on the crown of his penis, its heat penetrating the very centre of her. And at exactly the moment her orgasm rippled out from this spot, his dick jerked against the silky-soft core of her body and flooded her with warm sticky fluid. This time she screamed. He had sensitised every part of her sex, making it vulnerable to this attack and exposed nerves that had not been activated before. Raw feelings took her orgasm to new heights, her whole body concentrating around this single event.

In time he rolled off her. Gradually, very gradually, she became aware of more mundane things like the fact that her clothes were clinging to her uncomfortably, and that she was hot. The crotch of her panties, pulled into a thin string, were cutting into her.

'God, Duncan, that was wonderful,' she said. She sat up and unbuttoned her dress, pulling it off her shoulders. Her black bra had been pushed up above her firm, round breasts.

'I know,' he said, grinning.

'I've got to use the bathroom.'

'That door,' he said, indicating a stripped pine door. 'Don't be long.'

Kate got up off the bed with an effort and walked unsteadily toward the bathroom. She had barely noticed the decor. The bedroom was wallpapered in a flowery print with a light blue carpet. There were two or three water-coloured landscapes on the wall, and a large built-in wardrobe.

The bathroom was tiled in small white tiles with a white bathroom suite. On the glass shelf above the wash-basin was a glass with a single toothbrush.

Kate stripped off her clothes, used the toilet, then ran some water and wiped her body down with a face cloth. She stared into the mirror. Her eyes stared back at her, still slightly glazed from the aftermath of such shattering and repeated orgasms.

Duncan was lying on the bed when she walked back into the bedroom. He was naked. His body was athletic, all the sets of muscles well defined, particularly his abdominals which were flat and hard. His cock was still partially erect, its glans circumcised. He had a mat of thick hair on his chest.

'My turn,' he said. He bounced up off the bed, kissed her on the cheek as he passed her and closed the bathroom door behind him.

Kate tried to smoothe the creases out of her dress, stretching it over a small boudoir chair, then sat on the bed and looked around the room. The bedroom was neat with not a thing out of place. Well, almost nothing. That's when she noticed it. At the foot of the bed, peeking out from under the valance that matched the counterpane, was a scrap of white lace.

Unable to control her curiosity, Kate stooped down and pulled the lace out from under the bed. A very revealing white silk négligé had clearly been stuffed unceremoniously under the bed. She lifted the valance. There was a pair of white satin open-toed slippers too.

'Do you want a drink?' Duncan shouted from the bathroom. 'I've got champagne in the fridge.'

'No thanks,' she said. She heard the shower running. Why should he hide these items, she asked herself? Very quietly she got to her feet and went to the wardrobe. She opened the first door. There was a rack of men's suits. She opened the third door along. This time the clothes hanging from the rail all belonged to a woman. The floor of the wardrobe was racked with women's shoes.

Going back to the bed she opened the drawer of the bedside table. A silver-framed photograph stared back at her: Duncan with his arm around a pretty blonde in a black swimsuit.

Very calmly she picked up her clothes and climbed into them. Fully dressed again, she opened the bathroom door. Duncan was standing under a powerful shower, steam rising all around him.

'Who does this belong to, Duncan?' Kate asked, holding up the white silk négligé.

'What?' he said, looking astonished.

'Why did you lie to me?'

He turned off the single mixer tap. 'Look, I didn't . . . I mean I thought . . .'

'You thought if you told me you were still married and you wanted to fuck me in the marital bed I might not be so keen on the idea, is that it?'

'No. Yes. I didn't mean to . . .'

'Where is your wife?'

'Away on a course.' He smiled, trying to be ingratiating. 'Don't worry she won't be back till Monday. We've got all weekend. Or we could go to your house. Whatever . . .'

Kate took two steps forward. 'I don't sleep with married men,' she said. She reached forward, pulled the lever on the mixer tap full over so that a stream of cold water jetted over Duncan, then turned on her heels and marched out of the house.

Chapter Two

IT WAS RAINING. Hard. The rain bounced off the roofs and over-flowed the gutters. It had started in the middle of the night and continued all morning.

Kate had planned to do some gardening. The garden had been one of the reasons she'd bought the house in Kensington; it was long and narrow and had been carefully planted some years ago so the trees and shrubs were now mature. Though Kate employed a gardener to do most of the hard work, she liked to potter around at the weekend as a way of getting her mind off her most pressing cases.

But there was going to be no gardening today. Instead she sat in her kitchen, with her briefcase open on the kitchen table, and pored over her files. Unfortunately she found it difficult to concentrate, just as it had been difficult to sleep last night.

What Duncan Andrews had done to her rankled. At first she had been angry with him; then she had registered disgust at herself for being so gullible. By four o'clock in the morning she had begun to think about revenge. She was certainly going to withdraw the brief she had been working on with him and make sure no one else in her firm gave him any business. She contemplated marching up to his front door on Tuesday evening and confronting his wife.

Why any man would be turned on by such circumstances she did not know, but she was certain that taking her to his house and fucking her on the marital bed was all part of Duncan's warped sexuality. She was sure he'd done it before, salting his wife's things away so his victim wouldn't suspect. She wondered how many others there had been. She also resented the fact that he had been lining her up, clearly making the necessary arrangements at his house before he'd taken her out to dinner, expecting her to fall under his spell.

The trouble was, as the rain had pounded on her roof, and she'd lain awake, that was not all that she had felt. There was another set of feelings entirely, feelings that emanated in strong, surging pulses from her clitoris and vagina, not to mention little trills of pleasure from her nipples. Despite all her anger and disappointment, Duncan Andrews had set her body alight, and she found it impossible to put out the flames.

Eventually she had slept. She had got up late and made a large pot of coffee which she still hadn't finished. But as she sat at the kitchen table trying to read through the depositions of evidence in a case that was a week away from a court hearing, she found herself staring out of the window instead, watching the rain splashing up off the paving stones on the patio outside.

In the end, all the emotions Duncan had provoked had faded bar one. She was no longer angry or resentful or vengeful, but she was still terribly aroused. Her mind refused to think about anything else. It played and replayed the images of what had happened last night, like some gaudy pornographic film on a continuous loop. She kept feeling his tongue tormenting her clitoris so wonderfully and the way his fingers had thrust into both passages of her body. She kept seeing the picture of his cock impaled in her sex and the torn tights. She kept remembering the incredible impact as his cock had penetrated her, filling her so totally. She could conjure up the sensation of each orgasm, each different yet each essentially the same.

Sex had never played a very important part in Kate's life – not that she had any hang-ups about it. She had lost her virginity in a civilised way when she was sixteen to a man five years her senior. At university she had selected her lovers with care and had rarely been disappointed. Men had made love to her with kindness and consideration, indulging in foreplay, and doing everything a modern man was supposed to do. She, for her part, had never had any difficulty reaching orgasm.

But after she had got married her interest in sex had declined. Like all couples, she supposed, at the beginning Sean had made love to her frequently. But that had soon died away and his interest in her body seemed to have died too. She had no idea how long he'd been having an affair – or whether the man she had caught him with, the stunning looking transvestite, had been his first homosexual lover – but after six or seven months he had certainly shown little interest in sexual relations with her.

The fact was that this arrangement suited her. She hadn't particularly missed the sex. She hadn't needed it. All she had wanted was her career.

She wasn't sure whether last night had merely aroused emotions that had been hidden away, or created something new. What she was sure about was that she found it impossible to forget what had happened. She didn't want to forget it, either. For the first time in years, she realised what she had been missing.

Of course that realisation begged the question. Duncan Andrews was the first attractive man she had met since her divorce – in fact, long before her divorce. It was likely to be an equally long time before she'd meet another one. If she wanted sex, if she wanted to recapture the shattering feelings she had experienced last night, she would either have to visit Duncan again – something she was certainly not going to do – or find a wider circle of men. They were out there, after all. It wasn't as if they didn't exist. She saw men she was attracted to every day of the week, men she would be only too pleased to have carrying her off – literally – to bed. The trouble was she never met them.

That was the problem. In her career she had

always taken the view that all problems had a solution; it was a positive attitude that she thought was responsible for her success. Having defined her personal problem, she thought it was equally just a matter of finding the solution; though now, as the rain cascaded down her windows, she couldn't think for the life of her what it could be.

It was still raining on Monday morning. Kate Hailstone parked her BMW in the underground car park of the modern block of offices and took the lift up to the fifth floor. It was one of the privileges of her rank as a partner in Dyer and Freeman she really enjoyed, especially on a day like today.

She had got up early. There was a case conference at ten on one of her more important cases and she wanted to review the papers before the barristers and her clients arrived.

Her secretary, Sharon Harper – a petite blonde with an East End accent, a neat, slender figure and a bouncy personality – was already at her desk.

'Morning, Sharon,' she said.

'Hi, Ms Hailstone. Did you have a nice weekend?'

'Wet.' Kate didn't want to go into details. 'You?'

'Fabulous.' Sharon grinned from ear to ear and winked. Her expression left little doubt as to what she had been doing

'Can you bring me in the Antrim/Forstater file? The case conference is at ten.'

'It's right here,' Sharon said. A good secretary always anticipated her boss's requirements and

Sharon was one of the best. She handed Kate a bundle of files. 'Coffee?'

'Please.' Kate opened her office door. She had a small office which, like all the outer offices, had floor to ceiling plate-glass forming one wall affording spectacular views along Fleet Street. She sat in her leather swivel chair and put the file down in front of her. As she opened it she noticed Sharon had also handed her a newspaper in the same bundle. She pulled it out from under the file. It was the *City Times*, a give-away paper that was distributed throughout London.

'Coffee,' Sharon said, walking in and setting down a steaming mug on Kate's modern glass-topped desk.

'Is this yours?' Kate asked.

'Yes. Sorry, my mistake. I always pick it up on the way to work. I love reading 'Kindred Spirits'. It's a laugh. And sometimes ... Well, you know ...'

'Kindred Spirits'? What's that?'

'See for yourself. Middle section. It's a sort of lonely hearts, but a lot raunchier ... I mean, less prissy.'

Kate opened the paper. Printed across the centrefold were ten columns of small ads under the boldly printed title 'Kindred Spirits', with little cupids decorating the margins; their arrows, like the title, were highlighted in red. She read one of the ads. *Male, good-looking, fit and v.healthy n/s gsol. Loves to boogie. Wltm busty, fun loving brunette for nights of adult entertainment. Age not important. Voice*

28

mail 685 443.

'Do you use this?' Kate asked her secretary.

Sharon hesitated, blushing a light shade of pink. 'Well . . . It can be fun. Sometimes I just listen to the messages.'

'What do you mean?'

'If you call the voice mail, you can hear the guy's message and leave one of your own.'

'What, and then he calls you?'

'Yeah. Then you arrange to meet up. It's simple; no complications.'

'Do you do this often?'

Sharon blushed again, then grinned. 'The thing is, you see, you meet a different type of bloke. I mean, if you go down the disco you only meet all the usual Henries. This way, you can meet some really posh geezers. It's great.' She turned and went to the door. 'Is there anything else you want?'

'No, I'll plough on. Call me when they arrive.'

'Right.'

'Do you want this back?' Kate waved the paper.

'No, it's all right. I've read it.'

Sharon closed the door behind her. Kate stared at the double page spread. *Male, blond and blue eyes gsoh. Available week days only. Wltm petite blonde 20–30 for private pleasure. Satisfaction guaranteed. Voice mail 332 102.*

Kate folded the paper away quickly and opened the case files. She began reading but found it hard to concentrate. The pages of the *City Times* seemed to draw her eyes away from the double-spaced typing of the brief. She sipped her coffee and made a deliberate effort not to pick up the paper again.

She managed to get through a wad of depositions then glanced at her watch. It was nine-thirty. She opened a second file but her eyes caught the paper again. *Satisfaction guaranteed.* The words made her shiver and the feelings that Duncan Andrews had aroused were evident again. It appeared that her body was determined not to allow her to put sex on the back burner again.

Giving in to her curiosity, she picked up the paper and opened it at the centre pages. She had never realised that such sexually explicit advertising existed. She glanced down the page.

Male 38 seeks companion for dinner and dancing and the ultimate. Looks not important but must have gsoh and n/s. Long term commitment welcome. Voice mail 921 540.

Female 32. Good figure and likes fun. Looking for professional man, company director etc. to treat her in the manner she would like to become accustomed to. Voice mail 367 922.

Male 21. Health freak with body to match. Come and let me show you my biceps. Blondes and big breasts preferred. Voice mail 717 821.

Kate had a vision of a shining, oiled torso with rippling abdominals. The idea did not appeal.

She saw that the small ads were divided into three sections: singles hetero, singles homo, and couples. She began to read the latter.

She 40 AC/DC. He 43. Both smokers. Wltm couple or single women to join them in bed. All games considered. Can accommodate. Cleanliness guaranteed. Voice mail

443 865.

Kate was astonished. Some of the ads in 'Kindred Spirits' were from lonely hearts looking for new partners but it was quite clear that most had nothing to do with the desire to find a permanent mate. They were purely and simply advertisements for sex.

Young professional couple. First timers. She bi curious. Wltm bi female to coax and cajole. Husband's participation optional. Can accommodate week days only. Voice mail 021 941.

Husband 41. Wife 32, extremely busty. Looking for bi man to satisfy both. Genuine first time ad. No time wasters. S/M room available. Voice mail 001 287.

But it was an ad right at the bottom of this column that caught her attention. *Mid thirties couple. Husband dedicated TV. Wltm similar couple or single male TV for talk and fun. Wife stunning, slim brunette. Voice mail 412 751.*

An image of the bewigged brunette in his black satin basque and stocking-sheathed shaven legs popped into Kate's mind. She imagined the couple waiting for the arrival of their guest, the man decked out in his finest lingerie.

The phone on her desk rang, startling her. 'Kate, they're here,' Sharon said.

'Oh, right.' Kate looked at her watch again. It was ten twenty. She folded the *City Times* up quickly and slipped it into her bag. She had only got through half the files and was going to have to wing most of the meeting. Still, she had done it before. She got to her feet, picked up the files and

31

walked into the conference room, trying to ignore the odd prickly excitement she felt in the pit of her stomach.

'Hello, you are through to the *City Times* voice mail service. Use your touch-tone phone to dial the number in the advertisement and you will hear the subscriber's message. If you want to leave a message for the subscriber, wait until you hear a three beep tone. Thank you for using our service.'

Kate had spent the last hour reading through the small ads. She had been thinking about them all day, but had resisted the temptation to look at the ads again until she got home. Now she sat at her kitchen table with the double page spread open in front of her and the ads she had chosen circled in black biro.

Male 37. N/s. Fit gsol, finding it hard to cope with the human jungle. Wltm a female guide. Long term optional. Voice mail 444 101.

Kate punched the numbers into the phone. There was a sharp click and a hiss of static.

'Hi. Thanks for ringing.' The voice was deep, relaxed and self-deprecating. 'I think you know what I mean when I say it just seems the most difficult thing in the world to meet the right person. Ironic really, when there are so many single people around, but friends represent a very limited circle and work is the same. So if you want to break out of the mould like I do, why don't you leave a message? Incidentally, I suppose I should describe myself. I'm tall, slender, with curly black hair and dark brown eyes. I don't think I've got any monstrous carbuncles anywhere. My name's Tom, by the way. Thank you for calling.'

There were three long beeps.

Kate took a deep breath. 'Oh, hi, my name is Kate. I'm ... Er ...' The plan hadn't been to say anything. She had decided to ring just to hear one or two of the ads, really to satisfy her curiosity as much as anything else. But the man's voice had sounded so sympathetic she found herself stammering out a message. 'I ... I've never done this before, as you'll gather from the very amateur way I'm sounding ... I'm thirty-two ... divorced ... brunette ... slender ... What else? I agree with you about how difficult it is to find new contacts. I'd like you to call me.' She gave her telephone number then put the phone down as if it had suddenly become too hot to handle. She stared at it, her face red and her breath short.

'Blast,' she said aloud. She had not handled that at all well. She couldn't even remember what she'd said. Had she given her name?

She stood up then sat down again. She wished she'd called one of the other ads first. Human Jungle Man was the one she'd liked most and now she had probably blown it.

The second ad she had picked out was at the bottom of the page. *Male 30 looking for no strings relationship. Gsoh essential but looks not. I like to please. Voice mail 154 290.*

She picked up the phone again and dialled the

City Times voice mail number, then punched in the second set of numbers on one of the ads she had selected.

'Hi, sweetie.' The voice was light and smarmy. 'Just knew you'd have to call. My name's Craig and, sister, I can tell you I'm really built and I can give you the best time you've ever had bar none. I'm the business. So don't hesitate, sweetie. Give yourself a break and leave a nice sexy message and I'll get right back to you. Service with a smile.'

Kate slammed the phone down in disgust. His advertisement had sounded self-assured, which was a quality she liked, but on the phone his self-assurance had turned to arrogance. She imagined he spent most of his day in front of a mirror.

She had ringed one of the ads in the couples section. The idea of a couple recruiting the services of another couple for what was usually described as 'adult fun' was of no interest to her but the ad that had caught her eye had stirred a sort of sickly excitement that she had found difficult to forget. Her curiosity – a quality much in evidence these days it seemed – made her dial the *City Times* number for a third time.

'Hello.' It was a woman's voice this time. 'Thank you for calling.' Her tone was businesslike. 'As we said in our ad, we are both in our thirties and have been married for ten years with no children. We like to explore the sexual side of our relationship and are looking for a single girl who feels, as we do, that sex is not something that should be confined to one-on-one relationships and who is bisexual or bi-curious.' The woman sounded as if she were reading from a prepared speech. 'If you feel like finding out who you really are, leave a message after the tone.'

Kate hung up. She got up from the table and took a bottle of white wine from the fridge, taking off the rubber stopper that kept it fresh and pouring herself a glass. The last message had given her that unnerving tingling sensation in the pit of her stomach. The woman had sounded confident and assured, knowing what she wanted and exactly how to get it. Kate couldn't help wishing she could be that straightforward when it came to sex.

Sipping the wine, she walked upstairs. She had scanned the small ads as soon as she'd got home, interrupting her normal routine, and she had not yet showered. Stripping off the smart grey suit she wore for work, she turned on the mixer taps in the shower cubicle. When she had bought the house, she'd had a number of alterations made, and one of them was installing a powerful German-made shower in a separate glass shower cubicle. She stood under the jet of water for a long time, her mind in neutral, not consciously thinking about anything.

As she towelled herself dry, she caught sight of her naked body in the long mirror on the bathroom wall. She imagined the man with the deep voice waiting for her in her bedroom. Neither could she forget the cool, calculated tone of the woman's voice. She examined her body in the glass. Her breasts were round and full with only the thinnest band of areola around the nipples that the water had made erect. Her belly was flat and her jet black pubic hair not the usual triangular shape but more like a fat cigar extending up from the apex of her thighs.

Tentatively, she ran her hand over the curves of her right breast. She rubbed her palm across the nipple and felt a little tingle of sensation. In the mirror she watched her hand travel down to her pubes. She stroked them gently, as though she were stroking a frightened animal, and produced a second, very muted, flutter of pleasure.

Kate walked through into her bedroom. It was a pleasant room facing the garden at the back of the house. She had the luxury of a separate dressing room next door – another of her alterations – so it was uncluttered by wardrobes and chest of drawers. There was a large double bed, two bedside chests, a small button-backed sofa and a television discreetly tucked into the corner. The walls were oatmeal and the carpet cream; she had hung some of her collection of pictures on the walls, mostly colourful abstracts. One, immediately opposite the foot of the bed, was a complex tangle of impressionistic heads and limbs in vivid colours, scarlet and bright blue; a single pair of eyes dominated the whole, their expression unmistakably sardonic.

She lay on the cream bedclothes. The silk of the counterpane felt deliciously cool against her skin. It was still hot outside, the summer sun returning after the rain of the weekend, but the bedroom was north-facing and was the coldest room in the house.

Kate parted her legs slowly. She didn't think she had ever been so conscious of her sex. It was as if, as her thighs parted, she could feel her labia parting too. The sensation made her clitoris pulse. It had been like this all weekend. Whatever Duncan Andrews had done to her, the effect showed no signs of wearing off.

She rolled onto her stomach and pulled herself across the bed until she could reach the bottom drawer of the left-hand bedside chest. She'd just remembered something. Just after her divorce, one of her friends had arrived at her door with a small rectangular gift-wrapped box and a bottle of champagne. She'd opened the box to find it was a cream-coloured vibrator. Sarah, her friend, had told her it was a replacement for Sean – more reliable, more pleasurable and a great deal less trouble. They had both laughed over it. It was exactly the right gesture and had helped Kate a lot. As much as her marriage to Sean had been over before she'd found him in bed with his transvestite, the experience had inevitably been painful.

Up until this moment, the vibrator had remained unused. Kate wasn't even sure why she'd kept it. But she had and, as she opened the drawer, there it was, still in its box.

She took it out and dropped it on the bed. Taking the long plastic tube out of the box, she turned the gnarled knob at the end to switch on the power. Nothing happened. The batteries were obviously dead. She unscrewed the end and let the batteries full out. Fortunately they were the same size as the batteries that powered the remote control for the television. She quickly flicked the remote control open, pulled the batteries out and slid them into the vibrator. Screwing the end back on, she turned the gnarled control knob again. The vibrator sprung to life, buzzing loudly.

She touched the torpedo-shaped end against her left nipple. The vibration was strong enough to make her whole breast quiver. She moved it over to the right breast and pressed it into her nipple much harder this time, until the cream plastic was buried in her pliant flesh and the hum of the motor dropped a semitone. Little pulses of feeling coursed through her.

She had masturbated before, but never with any great regularity or conviction and never using a vibrator. Occasionally she had produced an orgasm but mostly, though she had come to a sort of climax, the feelings were so dull and unexciting it did not encourage her to repeat the experience. Now it appeared her body had different ideas. It had never felt like this.

She lay back on the bed, stretching her legs apart again. Slowly, almost teasingly, she trailed the tip of the vibrator down her body. She felt her clitoris throb in anticipation and smiled to herself. She might not be at all sure what she was doing, but her body seemed to know exactly what it wanted.

With the fingers of her right hand, she parted her thick puffy labia. It was no surprise to her that she was already wet. She thought she had felt her sex liquefy as she stood in the bathroom. Her clitoris throbbed again.

She ran the vibrator over her belly and allowed it to dally in the cigar-shaped bush of pubic hair. Then she pushed it down and inward. The smooth cream plastic nosed into her open labia. Immediately she felt a sharp pulse of pleasure, her clitoris spasming wildly as the strong vibrations powered through it. She gasped. Reflexively she scissored her legs together, trapping the dildo in her labia, concentrating the vibrations on her clitoris.

A whole panoply of sexual pleasure rocked through her. She moaned again. She had never been a noisy lover. She couldn't ever remember making the sort of noises she had made with Duncan but now she found she was doing exactly the same thing. Even more extraordinary was the fact that, in this short space of time, she felt all the familiar precursors of orgasm playing through her body.

She opened her legs again, reducing the pressure on her clitoris, then ran her hand under her thigh and up between her legs. She felt the heat of her sex. She knew what she wanted now. Despite the way he had treated her, she couldn't stop thinking about Duncan and what he had done to her. She pushed two fingers into the entrance of her vagina, feeling the silky wet flesh part to admit them.

'Oh yes,' she said aloud, as she slid her fingers into her sex as deep as they would go, straining until her knuckles were squashed against her labia. With her other hand she pressed the vibrator harder against her clitoris. Almost immediately she felt her orgasm building again. She couldn't stop it this time. It was all to do with the small ads, of course. All the things she had read – both this morning hurriedly, and at her leisure tonight – all the possibilities they represented and the fantasies she had consciously and subconsciously developed as she imagined what each of the men would be like and what they would do to her, had created a sexual pressure that had been building up all day. She had thought about the couples too, the idea of such a *ménage* undeniably exciting, an impression of it staring back at her from the painting on the bedroom wall. The painting had never seemed to have sexual implications before; now it was full of them.

The vibrations coursed through her, her clitoris spasming wildly. She moaned loudly, the noise exciting her, then came. A thousand images played through her head but one was uppermost. She saw a naked man lying on a bed next to a woman in a white négligé. It was Duncan and the woman in the silver framed photograph. 'Are you going to come and play with us?' he asked.

Kate's body arched off the bed, her muscles locked, a hard core of pleasure centred in her clitoris sending out wave after wave of exquisite sensation.

It was a long time before her body came down from the highs of its own creation. Even then it was subject to little tremors and thrills as she eased her fingers out of her vagina and moved the vibrator away from her clitoris.

And then, without even thinking about it, she turned the gnarled knob of the vibrator until the motor was at full power and jammed the plastic tube into her vagina, right up, so far up that the whole thing almost disappeared. She closed her legs, trapping it in place.

The vibrations rippled through her. She seized her breasts in her hands and pinched her nipples. She wanted more, she was greedy for more. The dildo was not as large as Duncan had been but at least it was hard and went deeper than her fingers. She found that by squeezing her thighs together she could push it deeper. Relaxing them allowed it to slip downwards slightly; squeezing rhythmically therefore created the impression of movement. It also put pressure on her already sensitised clitoris.

'Lovely,' she said aloud, pleased with herself.

She picked her breasts up by her nipples, elongating them into pyramids of flesh. Her body surged. The vibrations spread out from the depths of her body, touching nerves she never knew she had.

'You're not frightened, are you?' Duncan's wife asked, her voice cool and self-assured.

She was taking off the négligé. Duncan had a large erection. His wife knelt over and sucked it into her mouth. Kate could see the whole slit of her sex; it was covered with downy pubic hair.

Kate wrestled with the image, trying to think of something else, but it would not go away.

'Why don't you let me undress you?' the woman said.

Kate let her nipples go. Her breasts fell back on to her chest, quivering.

'No,' she said, as she saw the woman's hands reaching to touch her face. She could smell her musky perfume.

'Is that what you want?' the woman said.

'No.' Suddenly the vibrator seemed to buck inside her. Kate's vagina clenched around it, producing an avalanche of feelings. Her clitoris jerked against the confines of her labia and she came just as explosively as she had the first time, her body shuddering from head to toe.

It was at exactly at that moment that the phone rang.

She was breathing heavily as she reached across to the bedside table to answer it. 'Yes,' she said huskily, not yet fully in control of her voice.

'Hello, is that Kate?' It was a voice she recognised but not one she could place. 'Yes, who is this?'

'Tom.'

'Tom?' She didn't know a Tom. 'I'm sorry, you must have the wrong number.'

'Tom. You called my voice mail. Remember?'

'Oh, right . . .' Two shattering orgasms had wiped out her short-term memory. She tried to collect herself. 'Right. Sorry, I was doing something else. Sorry.'

'That's all right.' His voice was the same as it had sounded on the tape, calm and rich. 'You sound out of breath.'

'Just ran upstairs,' she lied. She sat up. The movement caused the dildo to shoot out of her sex, producing a huge wave of sensation that made her gasp loudly.

'Are you all right?' he asked with concern.

'Yes. Sorry.' She mustn't say sorry again. She tried to concentrate. She hadn't expected him to call so soon. 'Thanks for calling,' she said. 'It's nice to hear your voice.'

'Some people say it's my best feature.'

'It's very sexy.'

He laughed. 'Well, I hope I can live up to it. Listen, I wondered if we could meet? I'm not sure what the etiquette of all this is.'

'Is there one?'

'You haven't done this before, then?'

'Never.'

'Why now?'

'Because I've spent too much time on my own. I've decided I need to have some fun.'

'Shall we meet in a bar somewhere? I'll carry *The Times* and you can wear a red rose, something like that.'

'All right. There's a little place just around the corner from me. Café Prague, in Kensington High Street.'

'Perfect. I'm in Notting Hill. Can I ask you why you chose me?'

'Because you sounded right. Have you had a lot

43

of messages?'

'Ten.'

'Are you going to try them all?'

'No. Only you.'

She had no way of knowing that was the truth, but she believed it was.

'What about tomorrow?' he asked.

'No time like the present. Eight o'clock tomorrow night.'

'Done. Don't forget the rose.'

'Don't forget *The Times*.'

'I won't.'

They exchanged goodbyes.

Kate got to her feet. Her nerves were still tingling from her orgasms. She looked down at the cream plastic tube that lay in the middle of the bed. It was still wet. She had a momentary urge to cram it back inside her and carry on where she had left off.

Instead, she put on her cotton robe and went downstairs to get something to eat. Sex had always made her hungry.

Chapter Three

HE WAS SITTING at a corner table. He had ordered a bottle of champagne and it was sitting in an ice bucket on the table in front of him, next to two glasses and a copy of *The Times*.

'Tom?' She held up the single rose she had bought at the flower stall earlier in the day.

'Kate, hi! You look wonderful.'

She should. She had spent an unusually long time on her appearance. She was wearing a bright yellow sleeveless dress with a V-neck and a relatively short skirt. Her legs were sheathed in sheer champagne-coloured nylon and she wore matching yellow high heels.

She saw his eyes examining her critically as he got to his feet and took her hand. He shook it rather self-consciously.

'I ordered champagne. Or would you like something else?'

'Champagne is fine.'

Café Prague was a modern, minimalist establishment with a wooden floor, cream-coloured walls and tables and chairs made from plywood stained in primary colours and tubular steel.

Tom poured her wine as she sat down; his eyes followed the movement of her legs as she crossed them. 'Cheers,' he said. 'Here's to new beginnings.'

'I'll drink to that.'

They clinked glasses and sipped the wine.

'Well, where do we start?' he said. 'We established you'd never done this before.'

'And you have?'

'Only once.'

He was a very attractive man, Kate decided. His black hair was curly and thick. His face was rugged and looked weather-beaten, as though he were a gardener or a sailor. His eyes sparkled with amusement at their situation. She supposed she had expected to be disappointed. In fact, during the course of the day, she had become more and more sceptical about the whole idea. A man who needed to advertise in 'Kindred Spirits' was likely to prove dull, sad and unattractive. She couldn't have been more wrong. Evidently social mores had moved on. The huge explosion in divorce had meant the singles scene had become a growth industry, no longer confined to the misfits of society.

'What happened?'

'Oh, she was a pretty women, but I think she was looking for a rich husband. I wasn't rich enough. Or perhaps it wasn't that at all. Anyway, she didn't come back for more.'

'What are you looking for?' Kate asked.

'I'm not sure. I think I'll know it when I see it. What about you?'

'I haven't the faintest idea.' That wasn't strictly true, Kate realised suddenly. Actually, as she sat with a perfect but very attractive stranger, she realised that she knew exactly what she wanted and that surprised her. What she wanted was sex. She didn't even particularly want conversation. She certainly did not want a relationship.

As if he were reading her mind, he said, 'Of course, a lot of people who read the *City Times* are really just looking for sex.'

'Really?' she said. 'But not you?'

'I love sex. Don't get me wrong.'

'But?'

'I prefer to like the women I go to bed with.'

For some reason, Kate laughed. 'How long does that take?'

'In your case two or three minutes.' He grinned.

'Oh, good. So you mean I can have my wicked way with you right now?'

'I was joking.'

'Pity.'

'You actually mean that, don't you?'

What was the point in lying? she thought. 'If you want the truth, yes. You're an attractive man. We're both adults. I would just as rather spend two or three hours lying in bed with you as sitting here drinking champagne. Does that shock you?' It might not have shocked him, but Kate was astonished at her own decisiveness, because she hadn't planned what she was going to say. The fact that he

47

was a total stranger – that they had no history together, no mutual friends, family or business connections – meant she could behave without fear of recriminations. 'Are you intimidated by women taking the initiative? Or have you already put me down as a raving nymphomaniac?'

It was his turn to laugh. 'Neither.' He sipped his champagne. 'You're a very attractive woman. I'd love to take you to bed. Is that simple enough for you?'

'Yes.'

'But I'd like to know why, first.'

'Why?'

'This is not something you usually do, Kate. I can tell. You're not usually so . . .' He searched for the right word. 'Assertive with men. You're trying this approach like it's a new dress. You want to see if it suits you. That's probably the reason you called the voice mail: all part of a new approach. Am I right? So I'd like to know what's suddenly brought on this change.'

He was looking right into Kate's eyes. She felt a surge of excitement, imagining herself in bed with him. He was right. She had never been so forth-right with a man. 'It's a combination of things. I've been throwing myself into my work to get over a bad divorce. I suppose I didn't realise what I was missing. So I decided to do something about it.' That was more or less the truth, she thought.

'Interesting. And I happened to be the first?'

'Yes.'

'I'm flattered.'

'And you?'

'Why did I advertise in *City Times*? Because I never met anyone outside my circle of friends and I wanted to meet someone new. Simple as that.'

'For sex?'

'Yes. But not exclusively. I like meeting new people.'

'Are you married?'

'Like you, divorced.' He didn't expand on that and Kate wasn't in the mood to enquire further.

'Well, so far, to use your expression, the dress fits,' Kate said. 'I find it very refreshing to be so honest with a man.' It was exciting, too. In the past, Kate had always played the conventional game, waiting for the man to make the running. The fact that she was doing it for herself added an extra dimension to her arousal.

'Good. So what do you want to do?'

'I want you to take me to bed,' she said. 'So it's just a question of . . .'

He grinned. 'Your place or mine?'

'Mine's just around the corner.'

He picked up his glass and downed the champagne. 'We'll take the rest of it with us,' he said, summoning the waitress.

Kate's body was tingling. It was as though she'd had a mild electric shock. She showed him into her house. 'Do you mind if I don't give you the conducted tour?' she asked. She was behaving outrageously, she knew, but she found it totally exhilarating.

'No.'

'This way, then.'

'Glasses?' he said, holding up the bottle of champagne.

She took the bottle from his hand and set it down on the hall table. 'Later,' she said. She took his hand; it was cool to the touch. She led him to the foot of the stairs, then turned to face him. 'I'm in the mood to be very demanding,' she said.

He pulled her into his arms and kissed her on the mouth. His tongue plunged between her lips, hot and wet. She sucked on it.

'Demand away,' he said, smiling.

In her bedroom, she closed the door behind them. None of this had been planned. She had worn her best lingerie, though. She'd certainly thought that far ahead.

'Cosy,' he said. He caught her hand and pulled her into his arms again. He kissed her lightly on the lips this time.

'Will you do something for me?' she asked.

'Anything.'

'Just sit there. I want to show you something.' She indicated the small sofa.

'I might get very frustrated.' He kissed her lips again.

'Please . . .'

'If that's what you want.'

'It is.'

She realised she knew exactly what she wanted to do, even though as little as a minute ago it had never occurred to her.

Tom sat down and crossed his legs. He was wearing navy trousers and a white shirt. His shoes were loafers with a little tassel of leather on the toe. 'Is this what you want?' he asked quizzically.

Kate nodded. She turned her back on him then pushed the right shoulder-strap of the dress down over her arm. The left one followed. She pulled the dress down, then wriggled it over her hips until it fell to the floor.

'Very nice,' he said.

She was wearing a La Perla white silk teddy, the most expensive lingerie she had ever bought. Panels of the most delicate lace were inset at the hips and breasts; the legs were cut so high that the crease of her pelvis was visible. The champagne-coloured nylons were hold-ups with wide lacy welts. She never usually wore stockings but she'd found these in a drawer, a forgotten Christmas present.

She sat on the edge of the bed and looked at him. She could see his eyes roaming her body.

The cream plastic vibrator had been promoted to the top drawer of the bedside chest. She slid the drawer open and took it out. She had never behaved like this in her life, but the excitement of being in control, of taking her fate into her own hands and making her own decisions about what she wanted to do sexually, not waiting for the man to take the lead, was exhilarating. She wondered why it had taken her so long to wake up to the fact that this was what she needed.

'Is that what you wanted to show me?' he asked,

51

nodding towards the dildo. To give him credit, he appeared to be taking all this in his stride.

'I thought it might be interesting for you,' she said. She stood up and stripped off the white counterpane, only too aware of his eyes on her buttocks, where the thong-cut back of the teddy bisected her pert, apple-shaped bottom.

'You've got great legs,' he said.

Kate lay on the bed. She positioned herself squarely in the middle of it and spread her legs apart, bending them at the knee, the heels of her shoes rucking the white sheet. The sofa was positioned at the foot of the bed so he would have a perfect view up her long legs to the taut white silk that only partially covered her sex.

She ran both hands down her hips and over her thighs, stroking the flesh above the lacy welts of the stockings. It was as smooth as the silk of the teddy, the flesh dimpled at the top of her inner thigh. She stroked the stocking-tops, the contrast between the rather coarse texture of the lace and the smoothness of her skin very marked. It excited her. But then everything she was doing excited her. She could feel her clitoris throbbing almost continuously and her nipples were as hard as little chips of ice. She wondered if the dampness of her sex was visible to him, the white silk darkened by it.

Three metal poppers held the crotch of the teddy in place. She sprung them open one by one; the flap of silk fell away, exposing her sex. She watched his eyes examining it. He was a perfect stranger; she didn't even know his surname. Going to bed with Duncan without all the usual preliminaries had been a big step for her, but it was nothing compared to what she was doing now.

She raised her buttocks off the bed and spread her legs further apart. She felt her labia open. He would be able to see every intimate detail, the little pink lozenge of her clitoris, the dark scarlet tunnel of her vagina.

Kate reached over to the bedside table. She grasped the cream plastic phallus.

'Do you use that thing often?' he asked, his voice betraying his excitement.

'All the time,' she lied. 'I love it.'

She pushed the tip of the dildo down between her legs. As it nudged up against her clitoris she felt a shock of sensation that almost overwhelmed her. Up to this point it had been her mind that had generated most of her arousal; now her body took over. It was dry tinder waiting for a spark and this first touch ignited it. Whatever had happened to her, whatever had made her so bold and blatant, it had created a sexual facility that she could relish.

She pressed the dildo against her clitoris and turned the gnarled knob at the end. A loud humming filled the air as a second shock-wave rocked through her, making her whole body shudder. At this rate she would orgasm in seconds, but she didn't have the will-power to pull the dildo away. Quickly, wanting to enhance the feeling, she pushed her other hand up between her legs, her fingers jamming into her vagina.

'Oh, God ...' She raised her head to see his

53

reaction. The look of total lust in his eyes was the final straw. She bent her head back against the sheet, until it was almost at right angles to her spine as the wave of orgasm rolled up over her, sudden but not unexpected – the same feelings she had experienced last night, but amplified at least tenfold by his presence.

The force of her climax had closed her eyes. She opened them as the feelings ebbed away. Tom was looking at her and she could see a large erection tenting the front of his trousers.

Kate got to her feet, leaving the dildo lying on the bed. She walked over to the sofa and stood in front of him, her arms akimbo, her legs apart. The sweet musky aroma of sex had mixed with her perfume.

He looked up at her. 'Quite a show,' he said. He reached out with his right hand and touched her thigh. His hand stroked her flank, right up to the leg of the teddy. 'I really want to fuck you now, Kate.'

'First things, first,' she said, smiling, still enjoying being in control. She dropped to her knees. More wantoness. Was there no end to it?

She fumbled in the folds of his trousers for the zip of his fly. He made no attempt to stop her. As she pulled the zip down, his cock sprang out. He was wearing boxer shorts and his erection had already escaped their fly; he was circumcised, his glans very smooth and pink. Without any hesitation, she dipped her head and slipped him into her mouth, sucking hard. He moaned. She ran her tongue around the distinct ridge at the base of his glans. As she slid her mouth down over the whole length of him, she felt her sex contract. There seemed to be a direct connection between the two, the nerves in one provoked by the sensation in the other.

He reached down and took her head in his hands, pulling her away from him. 'That's nice, but I prefer the real thing,' he said.

'So do I,' she said earnestly.

Kate got to her feet. She walked back to the bed and sat on the edge of it as Tom began to peel his clothes off. His chest was broad but hairless. There wasn't an inch of fat on his belly. He pulled off his shoes and socks, then stripped off his trousers and boxer shorts. His cock stood out at right angles to his belly.

Kate's orgasm had left her hungry for more. She felt her sex throb again as she examined his naked body.

'Is it my turn now?' he asked.

'What does that mean?'

'I have a few ideas of my own.'

'Such as?'

He came over to her and sat beside her, wrapping his arm around her shoulder and kissing her hard on the lips. As his tongue thrust into her mouth, his hand cupped her right breast, his fingers scissoring around the puckered nipple. 'Lie back and think of England,' he said as he broke the kiss.

She did as she was told. Each stage of this

adventure had been a lesson in arousal. Now, as his hands guided her back on to the bed, every nerve in her body was tingling with anticipation. She remembered that extraordinary feeling as Duncan's penis had penetrated her and she wanted to feel that again quite desperately.

Tom knelt at her side, then leaned forward and kissed her left breast through the silk. He pulled the silk aside so he could get at her nipple, which he sucked into his mouth and tweaked with his teeth. He moved over to give the right nipple the same treatment.

'Lovely,' she said. Her hips were undulating unconsciously, taking a familiar rhythm.

His hands moved down her body, smoothing against the silk, then caressing her flesh. They stroked her thighs above the stocking tops. Oddly, the tight lace welt that held the stockings in place made the flesh above more sensitive.

The fingers of his right hand moved up to her labia. Very slowly she felt a finger delving in the wet, puffy flesh. When he found her swollen clitoris he pressed it back against the underlying bone and she moaned loudly. Then the finger rocked from side to side, not reducing the pressure but dragging the little nub of nerves with it.

Suddenly she felt something cold and hard prodding into her vagina. He had picked up the dildo and was thrusting it up into her.

'I want your cock,' she said.

'I know you do,' he replied, but pushed the plastic phallus in deeper. He turned the motor on. Kate felt the strong vibrations course through her, her sex clenching involuntarily around the hard object that produced them. At the same time Tom's finger began to brush over her clitoris very lightly but very fast. The two sensations immediately combined, arcing together. A third soon joined them as Tom leant forward and grasped her right nipple in his lips, sucking on it hard.

Kate moaned again, her body arching off the bed. She'd wanted his cock badly but this was making her climax – and beautifully. She had never felt so open, all her nerves exposed. His touch was perfect, the vibrations inside her spreading to her clitoris and tenderising it.

'You're making me come,' she muttered unnec- essarily; she was sure that he could see it for himself, every sinew of her body stretched out in front of him.

He pressed the dildo deeper. He opened his mouth and sucked her nipple harder, and a lot of her breast with it, flicking the little firm bud with his tongue.

She was coming. Her orgasm was centred in her clitoris and in her vagina too. She couldn't distin- guish between them any more. She was tossing her head from side to side, her eyes rolled back and her whole body trembling. She'd never felt anything like this. But at the exact moment her orgasm was born, as the wonderful sensations blossomed taking her over the brink into pure esctasy, Tom pulled the vibrator out of her and rolled onto her body, his big erection plunging into her sex.

Kate literally screamed. The contrast between the cold lifeless dildo and this hard throbbing cock was so marked and so wonderful that she experienced a whole new set of sensations on top of and in addition to the paroxysms of orgasm. Every feeling she had was magnified, elongated, enriched. She gasped for breath, the fire of her passion burning all the oxygen. Her orgasm went on for a long time, her arms and legs wrapping themselves around him as tightly as the muscles of her sex.

Somewhere in the mists of pleasure that swirled around her she became aware of the hard, hot rod of flesh that was still embedded inside her. It was moving, sliding up and down the silky wet tube of her sex, slowly but inexorably. Her hands slid down his naked back to his buttocks. She wanted his pleasure now. 'Come for me,' she whispered.

He didn't reply but his cock moved more quickly; she felt it throbbing inside her. She tried to open herself for him, wanting him to go deep, so she could feel his ejaculation right in the depths of her sex.

His chest crushed her breasts. His cock was so broad it had forced her labia apart, exposing her clitoris. The base of his penis knocked against it on his inward stroke and, as her body recovered from its exertions, each contact registered more strongly. He was relentless, his rhythm unflagging, his powerful body driving his cock deeper and deeper.

To her amazement, she realised that she was coming again. After what she had just been through, she wouldn't have believed it possible, but her clitoris was pulsing wildly and her vagina was rippling with sensation. The absolute regularity of his thrusts was driving her to the brink again.

She levered her sex up towards him, changing the angle and allowing him still deeper. But that was the last thing she could do consciously. As his cock thrust yet deeper and her clitoris spasmed, a third orgasm swept over her. Her whole body shuddered and rocked, trying to cope with this new passion. Suddenly, at the centre of the maelstrom, she felt his phallus jerk strongly inside her, burying itself in her for the last time. As her nerves registered the extremes of pleasure, the centre of her body turned to liquid as his ejaculation pulsed into her.

Neither of them moved. Eventually he rolled off her. He was smiling, a quizzical expression on his face. 'Did you get what you wanted?' he asked, stroking a finger across her cheek.

'Yes. Definitely,' she said. And it was perfectly true.

The conference took two hours. Jonathan St Leger Smythe was probably the most boring barrister in London, Kate thought. He won his cases by attrition, by wearing the other side down, the limit of their patience tested by his verbosity. Unfortunately he did not restrict his verbiage to court appearances and droned on endlessly as he strutted around his chambers in the Inner Temple.

Kate stared out of the window, wishing she hadn't taken on this case. Her client was suing an insurance company for non-payment of a claim under his building insurance; when subsidence had caused most of his home to collapse, the company claimed it was a pre-existing condition and should have been declared to them when the policy was issued. Smythe was an old friend of the plaintiff's family: James Alexander Harding had insisted on using him. And he would probably win. That didn't make the case conferences any more entertaining.

Smythe was a peacock as well as a bore. He wore a bright red silk brocade waistcoat that clashed with the yellow of his striped jacket and the mauve of his Dunhill tie. He wore an old-fashioned fob watch, the chain hanging down from his waistcoat pocket, which he consulted about every fifteen minutes, as if to emphasise that he was a very busy man.

Fortunately for Kate, who was finding it hard to concentrate, he repeated everything twice. What she missed the first time she could pick up the second. She hadn't had a lot of sleep last night. Tom had left at midnight but she'd found it impossible to sleep after that. Though her body was exhausted, her mind refused to simmer down. In between long convoluted explanations for what she had done, it insisted on playing and replaying everything that had happened with Tom – every feeling, every movement, every thrusting penetration. Not content with that, it appeared to want to rehash the events of Friday evening, comparing and contrasting the way she had felt with Duncan to the sensations Tom had evoked. She had always been over-analytical. When it came to her job, it was a definite advantage, but in her private life – particularly after what had happened to her in the last five days – it would probably have been better not to dwell on every detail and try to work out what it meant to her.

But she could not stop herself. In the morning it had been the same. Her mind continued to pick over the bones of last night. A case conference with Jonathan St Leger Smythe provided a perfect opportunity for more day dreams.

She could think of a lot of metaphors for what she had done. After so many years of mundane sexual pursuits, and quite a few months of complete celibacy, she supposed it was like a dam bursting, inundating everything in its path. It was like a wild animal taken into captivity then released, running riot in its pleasure at being free again.

'The main problem as I see it is the testimony of the builder who examined the house in 1994. We have to establish that he did not make any reference to subsidence in his report to you . . .'

Kate's body still tingled. She was intensely aware of her nipples as they rubbed against the silky nylon of her bra. Though she was sure she was imagining it, she felt as though her clitoris was permanently swollen and had pushed its way out from between her labia. The crotch of her panties seemed determined to rub against it, however she positioned herself, and several times during the day she had shifted in her chair, trying to dislodge it from such intimate contact – obviously without success.

There was one thing she had known from the moment Tom had walked out of her house. She was never going to go back to the way things had been sexually. She was never going to allow herself to be trapped into a life where sex was played in a very minor key. She supposed, if she had thought about it at all, that she had previously assumed her body was just not an instrument that responded well to sexual overtures. Now she realised it *was* capable of handling enormous crescendos and she determined to keep it extremely well-tuned and make sure it was played regularly.

James Alexander Harding had got to his feet. She stared at him as he held out his hand, not quite sure what had happened. It took her a minute to grasp the fact that the conference was over.

'Thank you for all your help, Kate,' Harding said. 'I'm sure we're going to win.'

'Oh, Kate, a minute of your time, if you would,' Smythe said as he too shook Harding's hand.

'I won't wait,' Harding added. 'Train to catch.'

'Of course,' Kate said.

As Harding closed the door behind him, Smythe came out from behind his desk and sat on the edge of it, in front of the large leather chair into which Kate was firmly wedged.

'Just a word,' he said, his voice suddenly more nervous.

'What is it, Jonathan?' She made no attempt to

be friendly. 'I've got to get back to my office.'

'Just wondered . . . just thought . . .'

Kate uncrossed her long legs. She wasn't in the mood for prevarication. 'Spit it out.'

'Well, we have known each other for a number of months, my dear. Good number of months. I just wondered if . . .'

'If what?'

'If you'd care to . . . well, the thing is, I'm doing a job on the North Eastern circuit. There's this lovely hotel just outside Sheffield where I always stay . . .' His face suddenly changed to a deep purple. 'Do a wonderful claret. And Stilton.'

'And?' Kate prompted, guessing what was coming next.

'Well, you know. We could have a nice dinner . . .'

Kate laughed. A week ago she would have left it at that, walked out of his office without a word. But circumstances had changed and she wanted to hear more.

'Go on, Jonathan,' she said, arching one eyebrow.

'I just . . .' The purple in his cheeks deepened. 'I mean, they have such lovely rooms.'

Kate stood up. She took one step toward him, so they were no more than a foot apart. 'Are you trying to tell me you want to fuck me, Jonathan? Is that it?'

'No! No. Well . . . Yes. But I mean . . . Not . . .'

'You're a sweetie, Jonathan.' She patted his cheek. 'But I really think that's a man's job.'

She managed to keep a straight face until she got

into the corridor outside, then allowed a grin to spread from ear to ear. Jonathan had never made any advances towards her before. She wondered if her experience last night had produced a new batch of phremones that had suddenly made him sniff a sexual agenda.

She was still grinning when she got back to her office.

'Hi, Kate,' Sharon said cheerily, as she walked through the general office. 'Two messages. Simpson and Notley and Janet Fraser. Not urgent. What's got into you?'

'Jonathan St Leger Smythe. Or rather, he would like to.'

'What, he made a pass at you?'

'I think I came somewhere between the Stilton and the port,' she said, imitating his pukka tones.

'Cor, the thought of it makes my skin crawl,' Sharon said.

'Me too. Give me ten minutes, then you can return those calls.'

Still grinning, Kate closed her office door behind her and put her briefcase on the desk. She sat in her swivel chair and opened the case, taking out her copy of the *City Times* and opening it at the centre page. She had decided what she was going to do this morning. If she really wanted to take control of her fate, replying to ads in 'Kindred Spirits' was not the answer. The voice mail system meant men would have to pick her on the basis of her message. What she needed to do was take an ad of her own. In that way she would be in control. She could do the picking.

She picked up the phone and punched in the number.

' 'Kindred Spirits'. Good afternoon, how may I help you?'

'Hello. I'd like to place an ad, please.'

'Which section, Miss?'

'Singles, hetero.'

'Right. That's ten pounds per line per week. Minimum two lines. Do you want voice mail or post box facilities?'

'I'm sorry?' Kate hadn't expected that question.

'Well, you can have the voice mail, which is like answerphone messages, or you can have a box number, where people reply to your ad by post. We collect all the replies and send them on to you.'

Kate hadn't realised this service was available and it appealed to her. She thought she had a better chance of assessing the candidates by mail than with short messages left over the telephone. 'Oh, right, I'll take a box number, then.'

'That's fifteen pounds plus one pound for each letter that you receive.'

'Fine.'

'Right. Can I have your credit card number and expiry date?'

Kate gave her the information.

'Now, if you'd like to dictate your message?'

Kate had composed the message in the middle of the night. She'd written it and rewritten it several times in her head. In the end, she'd decided to keep it simple and to the point. 'Attractive, slim brunette, 32, wants lovers not friends. No long-term involvement required,' she said slowly.

The girl read it back to her then added, 'We'll put "Please reply to Box No Blank" after that,' she said. 'How long do you want it to run?'

'Two editions.'

'Right.' The girl added up the total cost and told her it would be charged to her credit card. The *City Times* appeared once a week and the next edition was on Thursday. Her advertisement would be in it.

'Thank you,' Kate said.

'My pleasure,' the girl said and hung up.

It was as simple at that.

Chapter Four

SHE BUNCHED THE sheer black stocking into a little pocket then lifted her foot and wriggled her toes into it. Playing the material out over her long leg, she watched the way the shiny nylon encased her flesh, transforming it into sleek contoured uniformity. She pulled the stocking on to her thigh and clipped it into the two black suspenders that hung down from the lace suspender belt. The suspenders pulled the jet black welt of the stocking into a deep chevron on her thigh.

She had never owned a suspender belt before. She had gone shopping this morning and found a shop off Bond Street which stocked La Perla and several other equally seductive brands. She had spent a good hour trying on a whole range of lingerie and came out with two large shopping bags and an equally large bill. Other than the La Perla teddy, most of her underwear had been bought with strictly practical considerations in mind. Now she had a different agenda.

The suspender belt was silk and lace. It matched a three-quarter-cup plunge-fronted bra and a pair of thong-cut panties. She picked up the second stocking, rolled it over her leg, and clipped it into the suspenders. She was already wearing the bra. She thought about not bothering with the panties but then decided it would be sexier to feel them being pulled down her long legs.

She looked at her watch. Tom would be here in ten minutes. Quickly she tugged the panties on, smoothed them into place and checked her hair in the mirror. She dabbed her favourite perfume between her thighs and breasts, wrapped herself in a white satin robe – another purchase from her morning spending spree – and slipped into white satin high-heel slippers.

Downstairs, she opened a bottle of champagne and poured herself a glass. The *City Times* lay open on the kitchen table. As promised, her advertisement had appeared in the latest edition.

She took the champagne and two glasses through into the sitting room and sat on the large red sofa, facing the window. She crossed her legs. The stockings rasped against each other. For some reason the noise made her nipples pucker.

Tom had told her he would be out of town until Saturday, so she'd left a message on his machine asking him if he'd like to come around early on Saturday night. He'd rung her from Manchester to say he would love to. There had been no mention of dinner or any other euphemism. Both knew what was on the menu.

She supposed, in other circustances, Tom would have been a very good 'catch'. He was handsome and wonderful in bed. But she wanted more – not in terms of sexual satisfaction, but as a way of finding out more about herself. This area of her life had largely gone unexplored and she thought it was time she mapped every bit of territory. A relationship with one man would not fit the bill. She wanted to find out exactly what she was capable of. That's why she'd decided to take the ad. She wanted choice. She wanted to see what was out there. She wanted to cover the whole range of possibilities before she finally made her mind up – if she ever did – what she would settle for.

Meantime she was very glad to have Tom on hand.

The white satin had slipped off her legs and she stared down at her thigh, bisected by the black stocking-top, the white flesh above it softer and creamer than she'd ever seen it. The stockings were a symbol. Before, she would have dismissed them as impractical and frivolous. Now she realised that not only did she like the way they looked on her, they made her *feel* different, too. They made her feel wanton and available. She liked the scrambling desperate need she'd felt with Duncan, where nothing mattered but to get at each other, but she also liked the idea of more ritualistic sex where appearance and clothes played as big a part as desire and need.

Sitting here dressed like an expensive whore, waiting for her lover, excited her. So did the thought that he was coming for one reason and one reason alone: sex. She was used to having sex dressed up as something else, part of a more complex relationship. It was wonderfully refreshing and arousing to have it isolated and unencumbered.

She had spent her life thinking about her career, about the right decisions to make to get on, how to get important clients and win important cases. Now it was time to think about herself.

Her heart lurched as she saw him walk along the low wall at the front of her house and turn into the short path through her tiny front garden. She had to resist the temptation to run to the front door and fling it open before he rang the bell.

As calmly as she could, she waited. The door bell rang once. She got to her feet, batted a stray hair back into place in her carefully brushed coiffure and walked into the hall, intensely conscious of the way the suspenders bit into her thighs.

'Hi,' she said breezily as she opened the front door, though breezy was the last thing she felt.

'Hi.' He was staring at her white satin robe and the high heels. Had he expected her to be more conventionally dressed?

'I opened a bottle of champagne.'

'Sounds good.'

'Come through. You didn't see much of the house, last time.'

She led the way into the sitting room. It was a large square room with a big picture window overlooking her front garden. There was a working fireplace with a cast-iron grate and brass fire dogs, and two bookcases slotted into the alcoves on either side of it. The bookcases were jammed full of books. There was a stereo on the other wall, housed in a glass stand.

She poured the wine and handed it to him. They raised their glasses in silent salutation. He drank thirstily.

'Do you know, I didn't even ask what you did?' he said.

'Solicitor,' she replied, trying to make sure her tone of voice discouraged further enquiry. 'You?'

'Wine. You don't want to talk about that, though, do you?'

'If you want the truth, not really. It doesn't matter, does it?'

'Did I tell you you're a very beautiful woman, Kate?'

'I think you mentioned it. You're a very attractive man. I had a wonderful time with you. But then you know that, don't you?'

'We were good together.'

'I bought you a present.'

'What?'

'This . . .' She put down her wine-glass, unknotted the silk sash of her robe, then pulled the material off her shoulders. It whispered as it floated to the floor. 'What do you think?'

His eyes stared at her body. She saw them moving from the soft flesh that billowed out of the low-cut bra to her thighs and the tiny panties. She turned a hundred and eighty degrees, letting him

71

see the way the thong of the panties emerged from the deep cleft of her buttocks then ran up to a shallow triangle of material that perched above them, leaving most of her bottom bare. She glanced out of the window. With the curtains drawn back, anyone would be able to see inside, but she didn't care. In fact, perversely, the idea excited her.

Tom looked into her eyes. 'I was right about you, wasn't I?'

'About what, exactly?'

'About the fact that this is all new to you?'

She stepped into his arms. 'I'm not in the mood for talking, Tom. For Christ's sake, can't you see what I want?' She ran her fingers into his hair and pulled his head back by it, planting her mouth on his and kissing him hard, snaking her tongue into his mouth this time. She writhed her mouth against him as her body shuddered with arousal. She pulled his head back. 'God, I'm so turned on.' She kissed him again, as his arms wrapped around her body, caressing her near-naked back.

'Come here,' he said, breaking away. He caught her hand and led her over to the large red sofa. He pulled her down to sit on the edge of it, then knelt in front of her, spreading her legs apart with his hands. He ducked his shoulders under her thighs then straightened up, tilting her sex up towards him and making her fall back against the seat of the sofa as he dipped his head to her crotch.

Kate felt his hot breath on the narrow gusset of her panties. His fingers pulled the material aside and he pressed his mouth forward onto her labia.

Instantly she felt his tongue travelling up towards her clitoris. It found the little button of nerves and circled it very slowly.

'Delicious,' she said. She bent her legs, digging the heels of the slippers into his back and sliding forward so most of her buttocks were poised in mid-air.

Tom's fingers slid up under them. He found the slit of her sex and burrowed inward until his fingertips pried into the entrance of her vagina. He did not plunge them deeper but scissored them apart, stretching the flesh this way and that. It reacted with strong pulses of pleasure that were quite distinct from the more familiar sensations that emanated from her clitoris.

She felt a finger tentatively probing the little crater of her anus. To encourage him she pushed herself against it. The finger hardened, pressing against her sphincter. The ring of muscles did not resist for long and his finger slipped inside her. At the same time, he thrust into her vagina, pushing two fingers into it.

She looked down her body, her flesh banded by the black bra and panties, the long black suspenders stretched across her thighs, pulling her sheer nylon stockings taut, Tom's head poking up from the base on her mons. She wondered what Jonathan St Leger Smythe would think if he could see her now.

Tom was ploughing his fingers in and out of her body as his tongue played on her clitoris. He wasn't circling it any more but licking it, pushing

73

it up then dragging it all the way down again. Each pass created a symphony of sensations that harmonised perfectly with the feelings his fingers were producing inside her.

She closed her eyes. In the blackness she could concentrate on each feeling individually. She could feel her nipples rubbing against the silk of the bra, and the tightness of the waistband of the suspender belt and her panties. She could feel the thin membrane of her body that separated his fingers and the way her flesh clung to them, silky and wet. Her clitoris throbbed violently as he licked it. She was coming. He was coaxing an orgasm out of her already.

In the past – in what was rapidly becoming the dim and distant past, before Duncan and the major changes he seemed to have wrought in her life – she remembered her orgasms were often strived for and hard-won. Now she seemed capable of coming with the greatest of ease. She knew what it was. Then, sex had been a small part of a much larger picture. Now, she had isolated it and was concentrating on that one thing alone. The fact that she had dressed for sex, spent so much time on her appearance and on selecting the right lingerie and perfume, was all part of it. She had been aroused from the moment she had picked the silky garments from their wrappings.

'So good,' she said aloud. 'You're making me come.'

Her orgasm was not sharp and explosive. Instead it seemed to radiate outward quite slowly, but gathering momentum all the time, spreading an inescapable pleasure like a deep, penetrating heat. Kate let out a long soft moan, her heels digging into Tom's back, her hands stretched out at her side clutching at the cushions of the sofa for support.

Tom raised his head. 'Turn over,' he said quietly as he got to his feet.

Kate opened her eyes. Tom's large erection was sticking out. A tear of fluid had formed on the eye of his cock.

'What, like this?' She rolled over and knelt up on the sofa, pushing her bottom out at him, knowing the white flesh was framed by black stockings and suspender belt, and the thong of the panties that ran up between them. She wriggled her hips at him, enjoying her wantoness.

He reached forward and took the thin strap that formed the waistband of the panties in his hands, pulling it down over her rump. The crotch appeared reluctant to leave her sex and had to be tugged free. She raised her knees one by one so he could pull the black material down over them.

She looked over her shoulder. He was staring at the slit of her sex, her labia pouting out between her buttocks like a mouth, a thick-lipped vertical mouth.

He stepped forward. Kate felt a shock of pleasure as his cock butted into her sex.

'Are you going to fuck me, Tom?' she said, not because there was any doubt but because she wanted to hear herself say the words.

He replied by moving his cock down to her vagina. As his glans nosed into the wetness there she felt her flesh pursing round it, as if in a welcoming kiss.

He thrust forward forcefully. The whole length of his penis shot into her, the crown of his cock hitting the neck of her womb.

'Oh God, Tom . . .'

She wriggled her hips from side to side, feeling his cock moving around inside her. His hands caressed her buttocks then gripped them tightly as he pulled her back on him, increasing his penetration. She felt her sex clench round him.

'Open your legs,' he said, his voice husky and coarse.

Kate obeyed, moving her knees apart.

She felt his right hand gliding over her hip and down her belly. It moved over her pubic hair and into her labia. She gasped as his fingertip touched her clitoris. As before, the breadth of his cock had spread her labia apart and exposed it. His finger pressed it back against the underlying bone, producing a wave of feeling. He began to buck his hips, moving his hard, hot erection in and out of her as his finger manipulated her clitoris, pushing it this way and that.

The combination of the two sensations made her catch her breath. Once again her whole body shuddered under this double assault; her nerves were electrified.

Tom pounded into her, using his considerable strength to thrust his cock forward, his abdomen slapping against her buttocks. He reached forward with his left hand and prised open the clip of her bra. Her breasts fell out of the bra cups as his hand slid around to grasp them, one after the other, pinching her hard nipples.

The sharp pain turned instantly to intense pleasure. The pleasure migrated, travelling down to her sex, linking with the nerves in her clitoris and vagina. And suddenly the pleasure was no longer just a series of delightful sensations but concentrated and specific, a pounding beat that was only going to lead to one thing. Each slick movement of his erection brought it closer, her second orgasm inevitable now.

She looked over her shoulder at him. His body was arched over hers, the muscles of his abdomen stretched taut. His hips were dimpled as they drove his cock forward and his eyes were riveted on her buttocks.

All the feelings in Kate's body, all the wonderful pleasures, funnelled down to one spot just behind her clitoris. As his cock powered up into her vagina, her orgasm exploded, sending shards of incredible pleasure out in every direction; every muscle and sinew and nerve was stretched to the limit. Her vagina was convulsing and her clitoris was in spasm too.

Tom stopped, waiting for her orgasm to run its course.

'God, you have no idea what you do to me,' she said, when she was finally able to speak.

'I think I have a very good idea,' he said, smiling.

Kate twisted to one side, forcing his cock from her sex. 'Now I want to do something for you,' she said. She shifted round on the large sofa so she was lying full length across it. 'Stand up.'

He did as he was told. Kate reached out and wrapped her fist around his cock. It was hot and very wet. She slipped it between her lips, tasting her own juices. 'Do you like this?' she asked as her lips played over his glans.

By way of reply he knelt on the sofa and straddled her shoulders, his face towards her feet and his balls hanging at her chin. Eagerly she sucked his balls into her mouth and heard him groan. She ran her tongue around each testicle then used her hand to pull his cock down into her mouth. She swallowed it, feeling his hard flesh nosing into her throat. Her tongue licked the whole length of it, then she pulled it almost all the way out and sucked his glans hard.

His cock was throbbing. It had been a long time since a man had come in her mouth but that was exactly what she wanted. She wanted to taste his semen; she wanted to do everything and anything. She felt more turned on and more alive than she had for months, years even. This was like a new life. Every nerve in her body tingled and every second brought some new delight.

She pumped her mouth up and down on his long thick phallus, cupping his scrotum in her hands and jiggling his balls with her fingers. His cock jerked violently.

Suddenly he dropped forward, burying his head between her thighs. In an instant she felt his hot tongue against her clitoris. She hadn't wanted that; she'd wanted to please him unselfishly. But then she realised that it was exactly what she wanted. As the tip of his tongue slid across the tiny nub of nerves, it was as if he had completed a circle. Everything he felt in his cock, she felt equally in her clitoris; every surge and pulse of pleasure wound the circle tighter like the main spring of a watch.

She felt his cock swell and shudder just as her clitoris throbbed with feeling. She knew that he was going to come. But the extraordinary thing was that she knew equally that she would come again, too, and had to fight the rising tide of passion, trying to hold it back so she could concentrate on him. She sucked him deep and ran her tongue around the ridge of his glans as she squeezed his balls.

He throbbed. His muffled moan of pleasure produced a hot explosion of breath against her clitoris that took her closer to the brink she was struggling to ignore. His cock jerked in her mouth for a long moment, then seemed to go completely still. For the first time, his tongue stopped moving too. Then his penis jerked backward, and Kate felt a jet of hot semen flow into her throat. She had felt a direct connection between her mouth and her sex before and again the impact, the sheer sexual thrill of feeling jet after jet of liquid exploding from him, was routed straight to her vagina as though it were happening there too. Her quim began to spasm just as hard as Tom's cock had done; in less than a second, her whole body was rigid, her thighs locked around his cheeks. A third orgasm, sharp and hard and profound, washed over her.

It was a long time before they rolled off each other.

Kate had swallowed his semen gladly but a little had escaped from the corner of her mouth. She wiped it away with her finger then sucked her finger into her mouth.

A shadow flitted in front of the window, catching her eye. Had someone been watching them? She realised she didn't care.

The doorbell rang once.

Kate was in the bathroom. She pulled on a robe and ran downstairs.

'Hi, Ms Hailstone,' her cheery postman said, holding up a large brown envelope. 'Sorry to disturb you, but I can't get it through the door.'

'That's all right, Clyde. Thanks.'

'My pleasure.' He grinned and set off down the path.

It was Tuesday morning and Kate was already late for work. She took the packet through into the kitchen and threw it on the kitchen table, while she put on the coffee machine and poured herself a glass of orange juice.

As the coffee machine gurgled she sat at the

kitchen table and opened the packet; a pile of envelopes spilled out on to the wooden surface. She picked one of them up, a light blue envelope addressed in neat capital letters. It was addressed to the *City Times*, 8 Farringdon Rd, London EC. Her box number, Box 43, was written on the top left hand corner.

This was the first batch of replies to her advertisement. There were at least thirty of them. She'd never expected this many. She tore the blue envelope open. There was a single sheet of paper and a colour photograph. She looked at the picture and a slight, rather serious looking man with a mob of dark brown hair stared back at her. The letter read:

Dear Box 43,
Your advertisement sounded appealing. I love brunettes. I want a lover, too, and don't care about friends. I'm thirty and single and, if you would like to, please give me a ring at the above number. My photograph is enclosed. I do hope to hear from you, as I'm sure I could give you what you're looking for.
Bill.

The coffee machine stopped gurgling. Kate poured coffee into a mug and returned to the table. She picked up another envelope, white this time and addressed in a sprawling, almost illegible, hand. Fortunately, the letter itself was typed.
Hi Box 43,
Well, you really sound like something, lover.

Really something. I'd certainly like to be your lover. Me, I'm into sex. Really into it. I've got a real weapon, lover, and I know just what to do with it. No point being modest, is there? I can really make a woman sing. Pick me, hon, and we can make music together. Telephone whenever you're free. I'll be waiting.
Wayne.

A photograph had fallen out of the envelope, face down. Kate picked it up. There, in full colour, was a close-up of an erect penis, its glans slightly wider than the circumference of the shaft that supported it. Wrapped around the base of the penis was what was obviously a woman's hand. She wore a diamond ring and her fingernails were varnished bright red. The man's pubic hair was a ginger colour and the penis sprouted from a rather round belly.

She glanced at her watch. She should have been getting dressed ready for work. Instead she picked up another letter.

Hello, out there,
Look, I know you put yourself in the singles hetero column, but you know mistakes do happen, and not only mistakes. Some chicks who are looking for guys to give them a good time are doing it because no guy really has done just that, i.e. really given them what they wanted. But they haven't worked out that it's not just that they haven't found the right guy – they're playing around with the wrong

sex. Does that ring any bells? Have you thought
maybe a woman could give you what you're look-
ing for? Well, I'm here to tell you I'd love to try. I
could be the answer to your prayers, lover, I really
could. I'd touch you so softly, kiss you so sweetly;
you just wouldn't believe what I could do for you.
If you're in the mood to experiment, I'm here for
you, lover. Just pick up the phone.
Pamela.

There was a photograph with this letter too.
Kate stared at it. The woman was a brunette, her
hair long and brushed out over her shoulders. She
looked like she was in her mid-thirties; she was
sitting in a comfortable armchair with her legs
crossed, wearing a smart black suit and a crisp
white blouse. The expression on her face was
quizzical, one eyebrow slightly raised; her dark
brown eyes looked straight into the camera. The
eyes appeared to stare at Kate.

Kate dropped the photograph back onto the
table and ran upstairs. She had an appointment at
ten and didn't want to keep her client waiting.

The day dragged. With her meeting over by
eleven, she had plenty to do, but found it impossible to forget about the pile of letters sitting on her
kitchen table. She'd thought about bringing them
in to work, locking her office door and going
through them one by one over a sandwich at
lunchtime. But she never locked her office door
and didn't want to have to explain to Sharon why

she'd done so for the first time.

Instead she tried to concentrate on her work and hoped that some drama might make the hours go more quickly. Often clients would ring with some urgent problem, an industrial accident or an insurance claim, that needed her to prepare and initiate immediate action. But none came. The day was totally uneventful.

At four-thirty she told Sharon she was going home early to catch up on some reading, and stuffed files into her briefcase to make it look authentic. In face, she hoped her evening might be a great deal more exciting.

As she drove her BMW home through the early evening traffic, which was thankfully lighter than she was used to, she kept seeing the photograph of the long-haired brunette. She could well see that if a woman had spent years enduring less than gratifying heterosexual sex, the letter might provoke a response among the women who advertised in 'Kindred Spirits'. Did she place herself in that category? Before the advent of Duncan and Tom, she might well have done. She wondered how many women Pamela had written to and how many she had succeeded in seducing. As she thought about it, she shivered.

She found a parking space almost outside her house; then she unlocked her front door. The letters lay in a heap on the kitchen table, the photograph of the erect penis staring up at her. She thought about going upstairs to shower but the letters seemed to draw her to the table like a magnet.

She collected a small waste bin from the sitting room then sat down at the table. She consigned the photograph of the penis and the letter that accompanied it to the bin.

She picked up a white envelope and ripped it open.

My dear,
I read your advertisement with interest. Like you,
I prefer to distinguish between lovers and friends,
nor do I have any desire for a longer-term rela-
tionship. The most telling thing I ever read about
sex was that the biggest sex organ of the body is
the brain. To me, sex is a cerebral activity as much
as it is physical. If you understand what I mean,
then it might interest you enough to want to give
me a ring.
Gerard.

There was a small head-and-shoulders photograph with the letter. It pictured a man in his late forties, wearing a very smart suit with a white shirt and a dark blue tie. He had a handsome face and short, very neat hair.

The next one was in another white envelope.

Hi Box 43,
Listen, lover, you sound great. Give me a ring.
Don't really need to say much, 'cause I'm enclos-
ing a photo which shows you what I'm about. If
you fancy what you see, I'll be hearing from you.
Adam.

Kate picked the photograph out of the envelope. A young man was lying on a single bed. Straddling his hips was a pretty naked blonde, her back turned to the camera. The young man's erection was framed between her thighs; he had his head raised and was looking straight into the camera, grinning broadly.

Kate opened five more envelopes, all from men, all enclosing pictures of their naked bodies in a sexually excited condition and all under the impression, more or less, that the photograph alone would make the recipient want to telephone them straightaway. In fact it had the reverse effect on Kate. None of the men, or their organs, attracted her.

There were seven letters from men who were clearly lonely hearts, their rather sad faces staring out from their photographs, their letters polite but unexciting. Kate swept them all into the bin.

There were six or seven letters left. Kate chose a pink envelope, perhaps the most expensive paper of the lot. Inside there was a letter but no photograph.

Hello.
You may want to throw this letter away the moment you see that it is not from a single male wanting to be your lover but from a couple. My name is Marianne and my husband is Peter. I'm bisexual. When we got married, I didn't know I was into women; but then I had an affair with a lesbian and realised I could not live without that

excitement. Nor did I want to lose my husband. In order to save our marriage, we came to a compromise arrangement. I would only have other women if Peter was present.

As most of the women I wanted were not bisexual, that didn't seem exactly fair on him, so we decided he should also have other women, again on condition I was present at the time – a quid pro quo. *In this way, though strictly speaking both of us are unfaithful, there are no lies and no deceits, which in our opinion are what really destroy a marriage. It works very well. We have successfully used 'Kindred Spirits' to find partners for both of us. As your ad appeared in the hetero column we wanted to write to you to invite you to meet Peter. He is a caring and inspired lover. Since you are clearly not looking for commitment you might like to consider experimenting with my husband. I will, of course, be present – but very discreetly and quietly.*
It would be an adventure for all of us.
Peter and Marianne.

Kate read the letter twice. She got up from the table and poured herself a glass of white wine from the bottle in the fridge. She sipped it pensively and went back to the table. Putting the glass down, she opened another envelope.

Hi Box 43,
I'd like you to imagine what I would do to you. It would be better if you took this letter to bed – get

naked, in other words. Lie on your back. Are you doing that? Now look at the photograph. I'm walking towards the bed with my cock in my hand. But you can't have it yet. First, I'm going to rub it over every inch of your body. Then I'll suck your tits. Then I'm going to slip my mouth down between your legs and lick your little clit and your arsehole, and push my tongue up into your pussy. Only when I've done all that, only when you're begging for it, am I going to allow you to have what you really want. Only then am I going to take my big fat dick and slowly, ever so slowly, feed it into your tight little pussy.

Are you turned on, lover? Are you playing with yourself just thinking about it? Are you?

Think about how you want me to come – deep inside you or over your belly. Or do you want to suck it out of me. Ring me, lover, don't make yourself wait.

Angelo.

The photograph showed a thirty-year-old man with dark hair and a dark complexion in a sharp Italian suit. It looked like he hadn't shaved for twenty-four hours; he had stubble around his jaw.

Despite making her angry at the man's arrogance, the letter had also made Kate feel hot. She opened the rest of the envelopes and discarded another five. She made a small pile of the rest, then went upstairs to shower.

She pulled off her blouse and skirt and reached behind her back to unclip her bra. As her breasts escaped the bra cups, she saw in the bathroom mirror that her nipples were hard and red. It was not a surprise – nor was the fact that the crotch of her panties and her tights was distinctly damp.

She had worded the ad deliberately to suggest that she wasn't interested in finding a husband. What she wanted was sex; her experience with Tom had only increased that desire. The letters represented a whole shelf of sexual experiences: she only had to reach up and pluck off the one that appealed to her most.

She supposed the sensible thing to do was to go downstairs, sweep all the letters into the bin and resume her life as it had been before Duncan had invited her out to dinner. She should climb into the shower and let the water wash away her body heat and her excitement.

But she knew she had no intention of doing that. Not yet, at least.

Chapter Five

IT WAS ONE of the most expensive restaurants in London. The large room had a vaulted ceiling and the windows, draped in tasselled and ruched curtains, looked out on to a garden where the fading sun was replaced by strategically sited floodlights which illuminated the blooms for the diners. The tables were laid with pink linen table-cloths; there was a bouquet of white roses in the centre of each next to a Georgian candlestick. The flickering candles were reflected in the polished silver cutlery and created little prisms of light in the crystal glasses.

He ordered Dom Perignon rosé. It came with a silver salver of canapés: a spoonful of Beluga caviar on a tiny blini; a quail's egg in a case of puff pastry; and a sliver of *foie gras* on a round of brioche, one for each of them.

The champagne was delicious.

Kate was glad she had not under-dressed. When he suggested they meet at the Le Lion d'Or, she knew she could wear her most expensive outfit and was glad she had. The women on the tables around them were wearing St Laurent, Lagerfield and Chanel, but Kate's sleek black Gucci dress held its own. Its asymmetrical neckline revealed one delicate shoulder and clung to her body like a second skin, its skirt long but split to mid-thigh to give glimpses of her spectacular legs. She wore black suede high heels, a silver choker and the darkest red lipstick she could find.

Gerard appeared appropriately impressed. They ordered oysters and *filets de sole mousseline aux crevettes*, which was one of the restaurant's specialities.

'I hope you didn't mind me bringing you here,' he said, when he had ordered a bottle of Chassagne-Montrachet to go with the main course.

'Why should I mind?'

'Because you might think I was showing off.'

Gerard looked like his photograph. He was dapper and smart, his suit immaculate, his shirt silk and his shoes hand-made. He wore a Patek Phillipe watch and a small unostentatious gold signet ring on the little finger of his left hand.

'This is a beautiful place, Gerard. I love it.'

'Thank you. It's just that I didn't want to give the impression that I had not understood what you wanted. A lover not a friend, wasn't that the expression?'

She had called him at six o'clock. They had arranged to meet two hours later. She'd been ten minutes late. 'Yes.'

'And why is that? Am I allowed to ask?'

She smiled at him. 'No. But I'll tell you anyway. I have a very successful career and a failed marriage. I have spent most of my life working. I decided it was time I had some fun, no strings attached.'

'Sounds sensible.'

'No sensible it's not. That's the last thing I want. I've been sensible since I was in my teens.'

'What do you do for a living?'

'Solicitor. And you?'

'I import and export this and that. Very dull.'

'But profitable.'

The oysters arrived on large white plates, their shells buried in crushed ice.

'And sex – what about sex?' he asked as she squeezed a muslin-covered lemon over the oysters. He was staring at her intently.

'What about it?'

'Does it interest you?'

'It didn't in the past. Not really. I mean, I always enjoyed it, but it wasn't earth-shattering. Not until . . .'

'Until?'

She ate two oysters in quick succession. They were delicious. She folded a slice of the brown bread that had come with them and ate that too. 'I met a man who aroused something in me that I didn't know was there.' That was the truth, after all.

'But?'

'Sorry?'

'If I had aroused such passions in a woman for

the first time, I might expect her to be clinging and possessive.'

'I suppose so. He was married and I don't go out with married men. He lied to me so it let me off the hook.'

'And that's what made you take out the advertisement?'

'Yes. So tell me about you. I take it that this is not your first time?'

'No. I find it is a way of meeting women who may feel the same as I do.' He had a small mouth with rather thin lips. He smiled, revealing very regular and very white teeth – the result, Kate suspected, of a great deal of expensive dentistry. 'I have to confess my sexuality appears to be quite complex.'

'Complex?' Kate queried. 'In what way?'

'In many different ways. I have a very vivid imagination. I enjoy exercising it.'

'I'm not sure I understand that.'

'Sex is always in the mind, as I tried to suggest in my letter. Excitement isn't just physical; it comes from doing things out of context, or experimenting with new ideas. I don't mean like the *Kama Sutra* – that is pure geometry.'

'But wouldn't a more permanent relationship give you—'

'With a stranger, there are no preconceptions and no inhibitions. With a friend, with anyone you know, there is a whole package of expectations and conventions that make it impossible to act spontaneously when it comes to sex. That's why I use

93

'Kindred Spirits'.'

'I see.' Kate had felt a similar freedom when she had first met Tom. She sipped the superb champagne and looked into Gerard's eyes. They were an icy blue. She still wasn't sure what to expect from him but there was something cool and calculating about the way he talked that excited her.

They finished their oysters and talked about nothing in particular over the sole. Only when that had been cleared away and Kate had refused a dessert did Gerard lean forward and put his hand over hers. 'You are a very beautiful woman, my dear.'

'Thank you,' she said.

'Tell me something: do you ever fantasise about sex?'

Kate thought about that for a moment. Oddly, the picture of the brunette with the long hair popped into her mind. She pushed it aside. 'Not really.'

'Do you masturbate?' He said it as casually as if he were asking her if she drove a car.

'I told you, I've been very neglectful of myself, sexually. The two go together, don't they – an elaborate fantasy and ritualistic masturbation?' The fact that he was a stranger made her feel completely uninhibited about discussing such matters. She would never have been able to talk this way to a friend.

'Yes.'

'Tell me about it.'

The waiter brought their coffee in tiny white

cups, and a tiered silver tray of elaborate *petits fours*.

'How interesting. It is usually the other way around.'

'What, you get women to tell you their fantasises?'

'Yes.'

'And then fulfil them?'

'Sometimes.'

'Like what?'

'Like a woman who fantasised about having sex in a public place.'

'Really?' Kate thought about the scene with Tom in front of her open curtains. Had someone watched the whole performance? She shivered.

'Are you cold?' he asked solicitously.

'No.'

'Actually, sex in public is quite a common fantasy among women.'

'Really? I can understand why. I suppose the constant fear of being caught gives everything an edge.' She wondered how she would have felt if she had come face-to-face with someone staring through her window as Tom had ploughed into her. 'And you . . . co-operated?'

'Yes. In this very location.'

'What, here?'

Gerard smiled. 'My dear, I think you are shocked. You should talk to the waiters. They will tell you it is a remarkably frequent occurrence. Of course, they are not supposed to have noticed, but it usually results in a large tip. Mostly, of course, it is just mutual petting . . . Though apparently they have discovered one or two couples fully . . . *engagé.'*

Kate felt her sex throb. She imagined Gerard thrusting his hand up under her skirt as she tried to maintain her composure. The idea was arousing. She could almost feel his fingers insinuating their way into her labia, edging towards her clitoris . . .

'The point is, it's what's up here—' he tapped his forehead '—that's important. The mind builds itself little pleasure goals. You say you don't have fantasies; that may be true, consciously, but unconsciously, I'm sure you will find they are there – little black holes of arousal waiting to suck you down into . . . infinity.'

'It's just a question of discovering them?'

'Precisely. And, since you don't have a starting point of your own I can make a few suggestions as to the games you might like to play.'

'Games?'

'On the other hand, I could run you home.'

It was her turn to touch Gerard's hand. 'I think that would be a shame.' In comparison to the strong physical attraction she had felt for Tom, her body's response to Gerard was muted. But he had managed to intrigue her, just as his letter had.

'In that case I will get the bill. Unless you'd like a liqueur of some kind?'

She shook her head, then swallowed the strong coffee in one gulp. 'I'm ready,' she said. Ready for what was another question.

As the *maître d'* held open the large glass door that fronted the restaurant, fervently wishing them a good evening, a burgundy red Rolls-Royce glided to a halt in front of them. A uniformed chauffeur raced out from behind the wheel and ran around the car to open the passenger door.

'This is nice,' Kate said as she settled into the deep leather seat and inhaled the strong aroma that only Rolls-Royces seemed to possess.

The driver got back behind the wheel. Though he was wearing a peaked cap Kate could see a fringe of blond hair at the nape of his neck. She could also see the way his eyes were examining her in the rear-view mirror. Very deliberately, she crossed her legs, letting the split in the skirt reveal a great deal of nylon-sheathed flesh. She was wearing very sheer and shiny tights. She was gratified to see the chauffeur readjust the rear-view mirror.

'Where to, sir?'

'Home, Philip, please.'

There was a glass panel between the front of the car and the passenger compartment. Gerard pressed a button in a small panel set in the armrest at his side and the panel closed, settling into its mounting with a dull clunk.

'I didn't ask you where you lived,' Kate said.

'Belgravia.'

It was a short drive. After a few minutes, the car pulled up outside a large detached house in a road parallel to Grosvenor Street. The house was probably Georgian, Kate thought, with a very symmetrical façade. Flowers and plants dripped from window boxes and hanging baskets, the double fuchsias in dark red and mauve highlighted as a bright security light snapped on.

The chauffeur raced around the car again and held the passenger door open. Kate saw there was a garage at one side of the house.

Gerard took out his keys and led her to the front door. 'Welcome to my humble home,' he said as the door swung open.

The hall floor was stripped oak, as was all the woodwork and the doors, the walls were painted a dark green. There was a staircase leading to a galleried landing and pictures hung under individual brass lamps. Kate thought she recognised a small Corot. In other circumstances, she might have liked to go through the house room by room, examining what would no doubt be a treasure trove of *objets d'art*. Gerard could obviously afford the best. But that was the last thing on her mind.

'So this is where you bring your victims, is it?' she asked, smiling.

'Victims?'

'Guinea pigs, then.'

He smiled. 'Is that what it feels like?'

'I'm not sure whether I'm supposed to play the spider or the fly.' She realised that, with the champagne and the white wine she had had quite a lot to drink. She felt slightly intoxicated.

'What would you prefer?'

'Why don't you show me where you keep your web.'

He took her hand and brought it up to his lips, staring straight into her eyes. 'This really is what you want?'

'Yes,' she said, without hesitation. It was exactly what she wanted. Part of her wished he had been like Duncan, pulling her into his arms and carrying her to bed, his desire so urgent that he couldn't even wait while she took off her clothes. Another part, the intellectually curious part, was just as aroused by the fact that he didn't. She hadn't the faintest idea what he intended to do with her, but from the conversation in the restaurant she very much doubted it was going to be like anything she'd experienced before.

He led her up to the first floor. There was a long corridor with a pair of doors to what was obviously the master bedroom. But he took her past these to another door at the far end. He took out his key ring again and unlocked it.

'My box of delights,' he said, indicating that she should go inside.

Kate walked through the door. Inside she found a small, square room. It had a white carpet and plain grey walls with no pictures and no furniture, apart from a large cupboard built into one wall, a double bed that had been positioned in the middle of the floor, and a small metal cabinet on castors with four or five drawers of different depths. The cabinet was positioned at the side of the bed. The bed was covered with a white sheet.

'Sit on the edge of the bed,' Gerard said, the tone of his voice changing.

'What are you going to do?'

He opened the top drawer in the metal cabinet and took out a wide strip of black silk. 'I'm going to blindfold you.'

For some reason these words sent a thrill through Kate's body that made her shiver. It did not occur to her for one minute to object. 'Why?'

He did not reply. He stretched the silk out between his hands and fitted it over her eyes. The material was so wide it covered most of her nose, too. As Gerard knotted the blindfold tightly Kate felt her pulse beginning to race.

Deprived of one sense, she found that the others immediately became more acute. She heard Gerard's footsteps crossing the room to the door. For the first time she smelt his aftershave, a flowery, sweet aroma. He was taking off his jacket. She thought she heard him undo his tie, the silk rasping as it was pulled through the knot.

'Stand up,' he said.

She did as she was told. Her sense of touch was enhanced too. She started as his hand touched her bare shoulder. It ran over her collar bone to her breast. The cut of the dress did not allow her to wear a bra. She felt his fingers exploring her soft flesh; her nipples were already erect. She had felt them both pucker the moment the blindfold had been applied.

'I have to take this off now,' he said.

His hands turned her round. She felt his fingers

on the zip. It ran from her shoulder blades to her bottom and rasped as he pulled it down. He wriggled the material down her body and over her hips, then allowed it to fall to the floor.

'Step out of it,' he said.

Kate stepped to the side. She heard him stooping to pick the dress up. She was standing in a strange room with a man she had known for three hours, in her tights and panties, with a strip of black silk covering her eyes. It was the most bizarre situation she had ever been in and yet it was terribly exciting. Any distinction between intellectual excitement – 'cerebral', had he called it? – and physical had entirely disappeared. Her body seemed to be trembling with arousal and anticipation.

'Now your tights,' he said. She felt his hands pulling at the waistband of the tights. He rolled them down to her ankles. 'Raise your leg,' he said. She raised her left leg, supporting herself by putting her hand out and groping around until she found his shoulder. He pulled her shoe off, then tugged off the left leg of the tights. The process was repeated with the right leg.

Her panties were black satin and miniscule, no more than two narrow triangles: one covering her mons and the other sitting at the top of her buttocks. She felt his hand stroke the material front and back. 'Sit down again.'

She felt the edge of the mattress against the back of her knees and sat down.

'Now lie back,' he said. He knelt on the bed

beside her, his hand guiding her until she was lying in the middle of the bed. She felt his weight lifting off the mattress and she heard the rustle of clothing. He was getting undressed.

'You see,' he said, the slight vibrato in his voice indicating his excitement, 'behind a blindfold you are anonymous. You cannot see yourself, so it is easy to convince yourself you cannot be seen. It enables you to behave without any inhibitions.'

She heard footsteps crossing the room to the door. The door opened and closed again. She listened intently, trying to hear if he was still in the room.

Something light brushed her body. It made her start. It floated down over her shoulders to her breasts, then caressed her nipples. It felt like silk. Her nipples became even more erect. They were so hard now, they felt cold.

The silk brushed her belly and her pubic hair, trailing down her thigh. She opened her legs, wanting to feel the silk against her labia. It glided down her left leg, all the way down to her ankle, then up her right, alongside the inside of her thigh. The crotch of her panties was no more than a thin ribbon of material and had buried itself in the crease of her sex, leaving her labia exposed. When the silk touched them, she gasped. She would never have believed such a feather-light contact could produce such a piquant sensation. She arched her sex up towards whatever was touching it, but it danced away.

She felt a weight settling on the edge of the bed

at her side again. 'As you have no fantasies of your own, I'm going to invent one for you.'

'Yes.' Her voice sound husky. She realised her breath had become short and panting. She imagined him looking at her near-naked body.

'Suppose I decided that I would get my pleasure tonight from seeing you lying here in my special room, while another man made love to you?'

'No!' she said at once, but the tone of her voice betrayed her. The idea excited her. He was right; the blindfold gave her complete anonymity and she was capable of anything.

'Suppose I had already invited this man in, that he was already standing by the foot of the bed looking at you? My chauffeur, for instance. He was interested in you, wasn't he? You saw him looking at you, didn't you?'

She did not reply.

'Didn't you?' he prompted.

'Yes.'

'Imagine that he was standing here looking at you in the way he looked at you in the car, standing at the foot of the bed. . . Those panties don't offer much protection, do they? He would be naked, of course. Can you picture that?'

Again she did not reply. Again, he prompted her. 'Can you?'

'Yes.'

She felt his weight lift off the bed. 'She has very thick labia, doesn't she, Philip?'

Kate held her breath. She didn't think anyone else had come into the room, but she couldn't be sure. The blackness behind the blindfold was total.

'And lovely breasts. Can you see how hard her nipples are? Like little cherries.'

Kate's clitoris was throbbing continuously. Her imagination was running riot.

'Take this, Kate.'

She heard one of the metal drawers being opened; then something was pressed into her left hand. It didn't take her long to work out what it was. The smooth plastic shaft was bigger than the one she had at home.

'What do you want me to do?' she asked.

'We want to watch you masturbate. Can you come like that?'

'Yes.'

'Good. Show us. Show both of us. Take your panties off first.'

Kate used her left hand to skin the panties down over her hips. The power of suggestion was so strong she thought she could hear another man's breathing. But that's what she wanted. The thought of two men – two naked men – watching her was incredibly arousing. She had never realised that she could respond to this sort of sexual experience – wild and terribly wicked – but it appeared that she could. She might have expected to feel at least some reservations lurching in the back of her mind, as she lay naked in this strange room, obeying the dictates of a total stranger, but the truth was that she felt none.

She spread her legs apart – wide apart – and angled her sex upward, wanting them to see every detail. She ran one hand down between her legs, cupping her whole sex, then used her fingers to hold her labia open. She was wet, soaking wet. With her other hand, she nudged the tip of the dildo against her clitoris.

'Turn it on for me,' she said.

A weight knelt on the bed. She tried to remember what the chauffeur had looked like. He was short and stocky with a very broad chest but he was quite young. She remembered the way his eyes had looked at her. She imagined his hand reaching out to twist the control at the base of the vibrator.

A hum filled the air. She gasped as the vibrations coursed through her clitoris.

'Does it feel good?'

'Yes.' In the blackness, the vibrations seemed to be stronger and affect her more profoundly. She pressed the vibrator hard against her and gasped as the sensations increased. She rolled her head from side to side, waves of pleasure rippling through her. She was going to come. Her nerves were already knitting together, preparing themselves for the impact.

She could see the two men in vivid detail, their large erections sticking out from below their bellies and their eyes riveted to her sex. Oddly, she could see herself too, stretched out on the bed, the vibrator jammed between her legs. For an instant, just the smallest fraction of an instant, she saw something else too, in her mind's eye: the picture of the long-haired brunette, her eyes looking steadily into the camera.

Then she arched her head back against the sheet and came, her body shuddering, a noise more like a sob of pain than a cry of pleasure rattling in her throat.

'Can you take us both?' Gerard's voice was quivering.

'No.' She didn't know what he meant.

'I think you can.'

'No.'

She felt a body moving between her legs. A hand took the dildo from her. Fingers reached out to caress her breasts, kneading the soft flesh. When it touched her nipples, the shock of feeling was so great she cried out loudly.

The hand traced down to her belly. It left a trail of sensation so distinct it was as though it had scratched her. It dallied in her pubic hair, smoothing the curls down against her mons. Her clitoris twitched.

'Tell me what you want, Kate,' he said.

'Can't you see?'

'You want both of us, don't you?'

'Yes.'

There was part of her that wanted to snatch the blindfold off and end this charade, but most of her was too high and too aroused to want to do any such thing. Gerard had been right. Her imagination had set her senses alight.

She felt the hand slide down into her labia. It pushed up against her clitoris. In the dark, every sensation was amplified, and this was no exception. Kate's clitoris seemed to tremble like a tuning fork that had just been struck. The finger rolled across it, then began to describe circles around it. Kate moaned and shuddered, stretching out across the bed. Was the chauffeur watching her, or was he doing the touching?

The hand moved away. She heard a drawer in the metal cabinet being opened again.

'Turn over.'

Her mind wasn't working properly. She couldn't work out what he meant. It was only when she felt his hands on her hips, pushing her over on to her side, that she realised what was required of her. She rolled on to her stomach.

'Got a nice neat arse, hasn't she, Philip?' The fantasy continued.

A hand caressed the pert curves of her buttocks.

'Up on your knees, Gerard said.

She obeyed mechanically as if she had gifted her will to him. She felt hands pulling her buttocks apart, then something cold and greasy was being rubbed into the little crater of her anus. A finger entered her and spread the cream inside, too.

Her body tensed. Were there really two men? Were they both going to take her at the same time? Because she could view it on the level of fantasy, because she didn't really believe there were two men, she found the idea extraordinarily arousing.

Hands gripped her buttocks tightly. She felt the unmistakable heat and hardness of an erection butting against her thigh. It moved upward, ignoring her vagina, and centring itself on the perfectly circular hole above it.

'No,' she said. This time she wasn't sure whether she meant it or not. Not surprisingly perhaps, considering the predilections she had discovered later, Sean had often tried to bugger her but the first time had proved so painful she had resisted his later attempts. But she felt different now. Totally different. In fact, her body was betraying her. As the cock pushed forward ever so gently, her sphincter immediately relaxed, putting up no resistance.

'Oh yes,' Gerard said. She felt him push forward. At least, she thought it was Gerard. As his glans buried itself inside her, she felt a wave of pain. Almost instantly it turned to pleasure, but not like any pleasure she had felt before. It was hot, scalding hot, a pleasure on the same frequency as pain and just as intense. Instantly it spread to her sex. Her clitoris spasmed violently.

He was reaching around to clutch her pendulous breasts with one hand, trying to crush them both back against her chest, as she felt his other groping around by her knee. Suddenly she felt the tip of the dildo sliding up her thigh.

She realised what he was going to do and she wanted it badly. She wriggled herself back on him, forcing his cock deeper and causing a new surge of that peculiar pleasure striated with pain. Her vagina clenched like a hand searching for something to grip.

The tip of the dildo nosed into her labia and started vibrating. Kate moaned loudly, throwing back her head. Her body was being swamped with sensations. She felt the dildo slipping lower, searching for her vagina. Though he was completely buried in her anus now, his pubic hair rubbing against her buttocks, she had the odd sensation of being empty, too. Not for long. The torpedo-shaped tip of the dildo found what it was looking for. In one smooth movement it plunged deep into her sex, right up into her, until the top was vibrating against her cervix.

'Oh, God . . .' Her whole body shuddered from head to toe. She had never felt like this. She was completely filled, completely stretched; every nerve in her sex screamed with sensation so extreme she wasn't sure whether it was pain or pleasure. No, that wasn't true. It *was* pleasure, but a pleasure that was off the scale of her experience.

The powerful vibrations of the dildo were making his cock vibrate, too; the two phalluses pressed against each other, only separated by the thinness of her membranes. The clitoris was experiencing the same phenomenon, quivering compulsively.

She supposed she had come the moment the dildo had thrust inside her. She supposed she had come again seconds later as the vibrations spread into every sexual nerve, but she couldn't tell. Her feelings were so extreme that she had no idea where one orgasm began and another ended. All she knew was that she was coming more or less continuously, her body racked by pleasure.

It wasn't only the physical stimulus. Her mind was joining in too, the silk pressing against her eyeballs to remind her of just how outrageously she was behaving. And the images she had conjured up earlier, the two men standing over her watching her masturbate, refused to go away. Would this be how it felt if there had been two men buried inside her? That thought only added to her excitement.

Suddenly she felt the cock in her rear swell and throb. As this created another enormous tremor of sensation in her sex, it jerked against the confines of the tight tube of flesh and ejaculated, pushing her own orgasm to new heights; her body registered every single spasm.

He did not move but she could hear him breathing hard, panting for breath. He must have released the dildo, because slowly it slid from her body, gravity and her own wetness making its progress inexorable. As it finally dropped to the sheet Kate let out a gasp, her vagina folding back on itself and her tortured nerves giving out a final frisson of pure pleasure. His cock softened and slipped away too, but by then her body was too enervated to react.

And that's when it happened. She felt the weight shift off the bed and, as she turned to relieve the pressure on her knees, she bumped her arm against a smooth, muscled thigh. For some reason she could not explain, she had the distinct impression that the limb did not belong to Gerard.

'Wait here,' Gerard said.

She sat on the edge of the bed, her heart pounding anew. Had Gerard really used his chauffeur?

She heard the door being opened. If she wanted to know the truth, she would have to whip the blindfold off quickly before it closed. Instead she remained motionless.

It was some minutes before the door opened again.

Footsteps walked up to the bed and fingers unknotted the black silk. She screwed her eyes up against the light. Gerard was standing in front of her in a dark blue cotton robe. He no longer had an erection. Naturally, they were alone.

He smiled at her, sat down beside her and kissed her on the mouth. It was only then that she realised that it was their first kiss.

Chapter Six

THE POST DROPPED through her letterbox as she was walking downstairs. It was another brown envelope, but not as big as the first. She picked it up and took it into the kitchen.

The night with Gerard had left her completely drained. She'd gone to work the next morning with the equivalent of a hangover – not from alcohol but from extreme excitement, which amounted to the same thing – then got home and fell asleep in front of the television by nine o'clock. She'd dragged herself to bed and slept for ten hours, then been startled awake by her alarm clock. Exactly the same thing had happened last night too, except this time she woke just before the alarm clock had gone off and, for the first time, she felt refreshed.

Friday was going to be a busy day. She was in court all morning and had a meeting with an insurance company to discuss a settlement in the afternoon.

As she made the coffee, the envelope stared up at her from the kitchen table. She made a determined effort to ignore it. She needed to concentrate today and she didn't want any distractions.

What had happened with Gerard had been exciting, there was no point denying that. But it had also been disturbing. The more she thought about it, the more she had convinced herself that it had been Gerard's chauffeur, and not Gerard, who had made love to her so forcefully, while Gerard watched. How he, in turn, had got his satisfaction – if he had – she did not know.

The point was not that she objected. She had no complaints. She had not been coerced. She could have torn the blindfold away at any moment and discovered the truth for herself. The point was that she had become so involved in the fantasy Gerard had created for her, that making any attempt to stop it was the last thing that had occurred to her. That was what worried her.

From what he had said in the restaurant, and from the way the room he had taken her to had been prepared, she was sure he had done this many times before. She was sure that the other women had been more forthcoming, detailing their sexual fantasises. How many included being blindfolded and fucked by the blond chauffeur, or by both men at the same time? What other items did the metal chest hold?

The thought made her shudder. She took her orange juice from the fridge and drank it down in two gulps, then took a cup of coffee over to the kitchen table and sat down. She pushed the envelope aside. It looked as if it contained five or six letters.

She drank her coffee and went back upstairs. She applied her usual workday make-up and wandered into her dressing room to choose an appropriately business-like outfit. She selected a navy blue suit. Stripping off her robe, she began to dress.

The impetus for sexual adventure had not diminished, she was sure of that. But, for the time being, she needed to pause. It was the equivalent of eating too much, she supposed. Having gorged herself, she needed to rest before thinking about another meal.

Though Gerard had told her about his 'games', she had had no idea what to expect. Having spent so little time thinking about sex, consigning it to the back burner of her life, it was a shock to meet people who had done the reverse and developed extremely sophisticated and complicated ways of gratifying their sexual impulses. As she thought about it, she realised that she *had* come across it before. The transvestite her husband Sean had been with was a prime example. His sexual needs could hardly have been more involved – having to dress as a woman, shave his legs and learn how to use make-up and wigs.

Her own needs seemed primitive in comparison, but perhaps that was precisely because she had spent so little time thinking about what would really turn her on. So far, everything that had happened to her had been exciting and exhilarating. But that didn't mean she hadn't enjoyed some things more than others – nor that she did not intend to expand her horizons further and find what else was on offer.

She pulled on the jacket of the suit and glanced in the mirror. For the last two days her eyes had looked tired and jaded. Now their sparkle had returned.

'Fifty thousand, and we'll agree not to go public.'

'We can't possibly go that far.'

'Then we'll see you in court – and it will all get very public.'

'We don't have any problem with that. Our clients have carried out a full and wide-ranging investigation and all the safety fences have been overhauled and brought up to industry-standard specifications.'

'If they had not done that,' Kate said testily, 'I can assure you I would have insisted on taking the case to court whatever your offer of settlement. The point is that they have an image to protect. If the public perceives that they had been so careless with their staff, they might also draw the conclusion that they were careless with their customers too – and for a major ferry company in a highly competitive business that is not good news.'

'Twenty-five thousand.'

'Twenty-five is ludicrous. This is a clear case of negligence. My client has lost a year of his life in hospital. Your offer doesn't even compensate for loss of earnings, let alone pain and suffering.'

'That's our last offer.'

'Fine.' Kate picked up the file in her lap, dropped it into her briefcase and got to her feet. 'Then we'll see you in court.'

'Thirty.' George Christie of Monarch Insurance sat behind his partner's Victorian desk. He had six double chins and a belly that looked as if it were just about to burst his shirt buttons.

'I'll see myself out.'

Kate got to the office door before he said, 'Forty.'

Settlements were like playing poker, with all the cards face up. But Kate was very good at bluffing. She opened the door and walked out into the busy general office outside. She kept walking.

George's big bulk lumbered after her. 'Forty-five.'

She got to the lift and pressed the call button, then turned and looked at him. 'I've given you my final offer, George. Take it or leave it.'

His eyes registered his exasperation. 'All right, damn you. I'll take it. Send me a letter confirming confidentiality and it's a deal.'

'I want the money by return of post,' Kate said.

'You'll get it.'

Kate smiled and extended her hand. 'Nice doing business with you, George,' she said, as they shook hands. It was like shaking hands with a wet fish.

The smile lasted for a long time. She had gone into the meeting with instructions from her client that he'd settle for twenty five thousand and she'd managed to double that.

She looked at the digital clock on the dashboard of her car. It was already five o'clock and there was no point going back to the office now. Instead she took out her mobile phone, told her client the good news, and drove home.

She was in the mood to celebrate. Unfortunately, the one man she would really liked to have celebrate with was away. Tom had told her he had to go to Australia for a week on a wine-buying trip. He'd left on Thursday. It was a great pity. Three or four hours in bed with him would have been an appropriate reward for her endeavours. She felt her sex throb as she remembered the last time she'd seen him.

Apparently her appetite had returned.

She parked her car and let herself into the house. In the kitchen, she took out a glass and opened a new bottle of white wine, raising it to her success.

The brown envelope stared up at her from the kitchen table. She picked it up and tore it open, emptying the contents onto the table top. There were five letters.

Sitting down, she ripped open the first. It was another lonely heart, a man who was looking for a woman to share the rest of his life with. The second letter was the same. The photograph was of a small bald man with an uneasy smile.

Kate sipped her wine. She opened the third letter in the pile.

Hi Box 43.
Start at the beginning. We're a couple. Yes, we know you're not looking for couples, but we just thought we'd write to say you don't know what

you're missing. You say you're looking for a lover – well, I'm that lover. I can give you just what you're looking for and then my wife can give you more. Much more. If you think you're getting great sex now, you wait till you've been to bed with the two of us. Different experience. OK, so it's a bit scary, but life's not a rehearsal, is it? Ring us, and we'll show you the time of your life.
Alan and Mandy

The photograph with the letter showed a tall blonde in a tiny red bikini, its bra struggling to contain two large breasts. A dark-haired man stood behind her, grinning, the fingers of his right hand tucked into the front of the bikini bottoms and distending the material.

Kate threw the letter aside. That was definitely not what she wanted. But it reminded her of the letter she'd received from a couple in the first batch of correspondence to her box number. She went upstairs. The letters she'd kept from the original consignment had been tucked away in the top drawer of her bedside chest. She sat on the bed, took the letter out and read it carefully again.

She had told Gerard that she had no sexual fantasies and that had been perfectly true. Now she closed her eyes and lay back on the bed, trying to imagine exactly what it would be like to walk into that couple's house, for the single and sole purpose of having sex with the husband while his wife watched. How would it feel to strip her clothes off in front of them both? She imagined lying on the bed next to him as he caressed her body, while his wife's eyes followed every movement. Would she be naked, too?

Kate realised her pulse had started to race. She sat up. The other letter was in the drawer, too. She took it out. The long-haired brunette stared back at her from the photograph, the quizzical expression on her face unchanged.

She reached for the phone on the bedside chest and punched in the number on the top of Peter and Marianne's letter. She punched it in quickly before she could change her mind.

'Hello?' The phone was answered on the second ring. It was a woman's voice.

'Is that Marianne?'

'Yes.'

Kate's heart was beating so fast it was difficult to catch her breath. 'Oh, hi, this is Box 43. You wrote to me.'

'Hello there. It's nice to hear your voice.' The woman sounded warm and welcoming. 'I hope you didn't mind us writing.'

'No. I wondered . . . I just wondered if we could meet.'

'Of course.'

'It's just that . . . I've never done anything like this before. Never ever. Would it be all right if we met just to talk?'

'Of course it would. In fact, that's what we'd suggest. Why don't you come over here? We can share a bottle of wine. You can see us and we can see you and if we all decide it seems like a bad idea, then no one gets offended.'

'I'd like that.'

'Good. When are you free?'

Kate tried to take a deep breath. The woman sounded friendly and sensible and a long weekend stretched ahead. Her victory over George Christie made her feel capable of anything. 'What about tonight?' she said, with her heart in her mouth.

'Fine. About eight? Let me give you the address.' She gave Kate the address and brief directions.

'I think I know it,' Kate said. It was a house in Fulham.

'By the way, what's your name?'

'Kate.'

'See you later then, Kate.'

Kate put down the phone. Her hand was trembling and she felt hot. She wasn't at all sure why she had done what she had done. It was another step down the road of her sexual emancipation. She hoped it would not be a step too far.

The house was modern and detached, built on a corner plot and surrounded by a surprisingly large garden, considering the lack of space allotted to the other houses in the development.

It was difficult to find somewhere to park, the roadside being crammed with cars, but Kate finally found a place around the corner. She locked her car and walked back towards the house feeling unbelievably selfconscious, her heart pounding. It was a feeling akin to going to the dentist, except that the nervousness was edged with a sickly excitement.

She was wearing a red summer dress with a box neckline, the white La Perla teddy, the white lace-topped hold-ups and spiky red high heels. It had taken her as long to decide what lingerie to wear as it had to decide on the dress.

There was a small wooden gate, set in a thick hedge, and a long path up to the front door. There was a bell push on the door jamb. Kate pressed it. A bell rang somewhere inside.

'Hi!'

The door was opened by a short but slender blonde. She was wearing a knee-length black linen dress with a mandarin collar, a narrow waist and a pencil skirt. She had a rather round but very pretty face with very large blue eyes, a small *retroussé* nose, and a sensual, fleshy mouth. Her long blonde hair had been tied into a pony tail. She extended her hand. 'I'm Marianne. And you must be Kate. Daunting, isn't it?'

'Very,' Kate said.

'Come in.'

Marianne led her through into the living room. It was large and rectangular with no fireplace; there was an ash block floor and the walls were painted white, with several dramatic and colourful abstract oil paintings hung on them. There were two identical dark green sofas in the middle of the room, facing each other, with a rectangular coffee table between them, its surface an inch-thick sheet of glass. The back part of the room contained a

121

dining table and chairs and French windows out on to the garden.

A tall slender man was sitting in the corner of one of the sofas. Though he was no more than thirty-five, his thick hair was entirely white. He was wearing a denim shirt and white trousers. The shirt was open at the neck and Kate could see that he had a mat of hair on his chest, most of which was white. His face was rather long with high cheekbones and vivid green eyes. He smiled and two dimples appeared on his cheeks.

'I'm Peter,' he said, getting up and shaking Kate's hand. His expression suggested he understood the absurdity of the situation but found it humorous. 'Would you like a drink? Red wine? Or something else?'

There was a bottle of wine on the table and three glasses.

'That will be fine,' Kate replied, indicating the wine.

'Sit down, please,' Marianne said. She sat on the sofa and poured three glasses of wine, pushing one over to Kate who sat on the sofa opposite. 'You said you'd never done this before. The first time is always the worst.'

'No, I think every time is pretty daunting. It takes a lot of courage. But it's a question of getting what you want out of life. That's what we feel,' Peter said. He had long legs and wasn't wearing socks in his light blue Docksider shoes. Kate found herself staring into his eyes. There were wrinkles at each corner that deepened as he smiled back at her.

'I just wanted to make an appearance,' he said getting to his feet. 'We find it's better if Marianne takes it from here. Unless there's anything you specifically want to ask me?'

He got to his feet with the lazy grace of a dancer. He had long fingers and manicured fingernails, the backs of his hands covered with blond hair. He looked at her steadily. She had the uncomfortable feeling that he already knew everything there was to know about her, all her secrets laid bare. He was the sort of man who gave the impression that whatever situation he found himself in, he would find a way of coping with it, that there was no problem that could not be solved. He eluded an ease and confidence that Kate found enormously attractive. When she did not reply to his question, he smiled and walked out into the corridor, taking his wine with him. He closed the door and Kate heard his footsteps mounting the stairs.

'How long have you been doing this?'

'Oh . . . Eighteen months. It was all down to me.' Marianne sat back on the sofa, kicked off her very high-heeled shoes, and drew her legs up under her. Her legs were encased in very sheer flesh-coloured nylons. 'I love Peter, I really do. As I said in the letter, it started as a way to save our marriage. I'm afraid I really went off the rails, at first.'

Kate sipped her wine and tried to relax. It wasn't easy. 'In what way?' she asked.

'Oh, it's a long story. I won't bore you with it. The thing was, I suppose it was something I'd always suppressed. When I thought about it, I realised I'd always had these really strong feelings for women – well, girls – when I was at school. I used to love them stroking and touching me. But it never occurred to me that it was a sexual thing.'

'So what happened?'

'I'm a graphic designer. One day, I was given an assignment to design a new logo for a fashion retailer. I went to see the woman who ran the business and she seduced me.'

'Really? How, exactly?'

'Very simple. She took one look at me and asked me if she could take me to bed. I was so shocked I just walked right out.'

'But?'

'I couldn't stop thinking about her. She was gorgeous. Tall, elegant and beautifully dressed. I had to go back to show her my designs. Her office was part of her apartment. I told her I'd been thinking about what she said. Ten minutes later, we were in bed together. She made me feel things I'd never felt before.'

'You said you went wild.'

'I did. I just couldn't get enough of it. I was even going around cruising gay bars at one time. But the odd thing was – the really odd thing was – that having a woman, being with a woman, left me with this really incredible desire to have a man. I used to come back to Peter absolutely ravenous for sex. Sometimes I'd just jump on him in the hall. It was incredible.'

'But you didn't go after other men?'

'No. Fortunately, Peter could take care of all my needs in that department. More wine?' Marianne uncurled herself and leant forward to pour more wine into both their glasses. 'Because my sexual energy was so high, he didn't suspect what I was doing, either. Not until one day, he came home early and found me in bed with my very beautiful red-haired assistant.'

'And then what?'

'Oh, divorce was really on the cards. Then Peter suggested that we compromise. What was sauce for the goose . . . That sort of thing.'

'And it works?'

'So far. It means sex is very high on our list of priorities. We both like it. If one of us was not highly sexed, I guess it wouldn't work at all, but we both are really into it, and that's what's made the difference. This way we can both get a huge variety of sexual experience and still stay together. Unconventional, but there are no rules, are there?'

'I suppose not.'

'So now tell me about you, Kate. What made you take an ad in 'Kindred Spirits'?'

'Me?' Kate decided she liked Marianne. Her openness was refreshing. 'I'd never really thought much about sex. I had my career. Then I found my husband in bed with . . .' She hesitated. 'With another man.'

'God!'

'A transvestite.'

Marianne laughed. It was a lovely warm sound. 'Really?'

'Black stockings, shaved legs, a brunette wig. He made quite an attractive-looking woman, actually.'

'That must have been a shock.'

'Yes, but that wasn't really what got me into . . .' she tried to think of the right word 'being more adventurous. A couple of weeks ago, I met this man. Something happened, I'm not even sure what. I realised what I was missing. And, being me, I was determined to make up for lost time. Does that make sense?'

'Of course. I imagine you got a lot of replies to your ad.'

'Yes. But mostly from men who were either lonely or thought they were so wonderful they only had to show me a photograph of their penises and I'd be so aroused that I wouldn't be able to resist.'

Marianne laughed again. 'I bet. Listen, I'm really glad you phoned.'

Kate realised her nervousness had disappeared. Her unease had been replaced by a growing excitement. 'Is it always this easy?' she asked.

'Easy?' Marianne looked puzzled.

'I mean, you've managed to make me feel as if this were perfectly normal.'

Marianne smiled. 'No. That's not anything I've done. It's just a natural rapport. Sometimes it happens and sometimes it doesn't.'

'So what are the rules?' Kate asked.

'Rules?'

'If I decide to go to bed with your husband.' Kate felt her pulse-rate increase.

'Oh. There aren't any. I mean, the only rule is that I'm in the room. Then I see what happens. There are no secrets. And no little lies afterwards.'

'And he does the same when you're . . .'

'Yes.'

'You just watch?'

'Yes.' The second affirmative was more hesitant than the first. 'So far, all the girls Peter's slept with have been straight. We haven't come across one who is – what's that expression they use in 'Kindred Spirits'? – bi-curious. Perhaps if we had . . .'

'Bi-curious?'

'Someone who wants to experiment with the same sex.'

'I've never done anything like this before,' Kate said. She realised she didn't know whether that was true or not. If Gerard had set her up with his chauffeur, this wouldn't be the first time she'd been part of a *ménage à trois*.

'But it doesn't scare you?'

'No.' She finished her wine. It seemed to have gone to her head. She felt slightly intoxicated. Or perhaps that had nothing to do with the wine.

'Do you want to talk to Peter again?'

'No. He's a very attractive man.'

'He's also a very good lover.'

'I think I'd like to find that out for myself,' Kate said coolly.

'Good. So that only leaves one question, doesn't it?'

'What's that?'

'When?'

Kate felt her heart flutter. There was a great deal of difference between talking about something and actually doing it. Perhaps a certain alarm was apparent on her face as Marianne said, 'Why don't you go home and think about it, then give us a call next week?'

'No,' Kate said decisively. She knew what she wanted. There was no point postponing the inevitable. 'I really don't want to go home, Marianne, if that's all right with you. I feel very relaxed and very . . .' Again, she couldn't think of the right word. 'Open. I was hoping I could stay.'

Marianne smiled. 'You are a very determined lady.'

'I found, in my career, forthrightness has always been the best way. It seems to have worked in my private life too, recently.'

'All right. This is what we do.' Marianne looked at her watch. 'Give it ten minutes. Think about it. If you change your mind, you can just walk out of the front door. No pressure. If you don't, then the bedroom's the second door on the left at the top of the stairs.' The blonde got to her feet. 'We'll be waiting.' Marianne smiled at her, touched her on the shoulder briefly then walked out of the door. Her footsteps mounted the stairs.

Kate stood and glanced at her watch. Eight-forty. She walked to the front window and looked out at the shrubbery in the front garden. Though her heart was beating so hard she could hear it in her eardrums, she felt perfectly calm. She remembered how she had felt with Tom, the first time – the feeling of being in control, of doing what *she* wanted to do. She was in control of her own fate again now and that excited her. She wondered if that was what had been missing in her early sex life: having to rely on men to take the initiative. All she had to do now was walk up those stairs. It was her choice.

She glanced at her watch. Eight-forty-nine. If she were honest with herself she knew she was going to stay from the moment she had set eyes on Peter. She supposed she should feel qualms about Marianne being in the room with them but she didn't.

Kate opened the sitting room door, walked into the hall and climbed the stairs. The second door on the left was ajar. Daylight had turned to twilight and she could see the last remnants of the sun through a large picture window overlooking the garden. She pushed the door open.

The bedroom was quite small. It was decorated in a rose-print wallpaper. The counterpane of the double bed had been stripped off and folded neatly over a chair. The curtains matched the wallpaper and were drawn back over the window, and the light came from the two bedside lamps with red shades that had been dimmed to provide a rosy glow.

Peter lay on the bed, his head propped up on two pillows. He was naked but his lower body was covered by a single pink sheet. Marianne was sitting next to him. She had taken off the dress and was wearing a tight, black satin body. The sheer flesh-coloured nylons were hold-ups with narrow welts that dug into her thighs. She was stroking her husband's erection, outlined under the sheet.

'Hi, again,' Peter said.

'You look comfortable,' Kate said, as calmly as she could.

'I feel it.'

For a moment, nothing happened, as if each of them were digesting the implications and consequences of Kate having walked through the door.

'If you'd like to use the bathroom?' Marianne said, finally breaking the spell. She indicated a door to the left of the bed.

Kate closed the bedroom door. 'No.' She smiled. 'But you could unzip me.'

'Of course.' Marianne got to her feet. She had taken off her high heels and appeared much shorter than she had downstairs.

Kate turned her back and felt the zip part as Marianne pulled it down. She wondered how often they had done this before.

She allowed the dress to drop to the floor then stepped out of it. Marianne picked it up and draped it over the chest of drawers.

'That's nice,' Marianne said. 'What lovely silk.'

'Love the hold-ups,' Peter said.

'We're into stockings, as you can see,' Marianne said. 'So much sexier. And more accessible.'

'Why don't you come and sit down with me?' Peter asked. Kate sat on the bed. 'You really are lovely,' he said. His hand stroked her knee. She turned toward him and put her hand up to his cheek, then leant forward and kissed him lightly on the lips, twice in quick succession. At the same time she ran her hand down the thick mat of hair on his chest.

'God, I wish I had tits like yours,' Marianne said.

'Gorgeous,' Peter muttered, looking down.

The white teddy was tight and cut low; Kate's breasts billowed out of the lace that formed the bodice. Peter's hand moved along her side, smoothing against the expensive silk, then cupped her right breast, squeezing the soft flesh. He wrapped his other arm around Kate's neck and pulled her down, kissing her hard on the lips, his tongue probing into her mouth.

Kate kissed him back, pressing her lips against his, feeling a surge of passion welling up in her body. All this talk of sex had made her hungry for the real thing. She pulled the sheet aside. Without breaking the kiss, she seized his erection in her fist. It was hot and very hard. She squeezed it and he moaned, the sound muffled by her own mouth.

Immediately he pushed his hand down between her legs, his fingers sliding against the silk crotch of the teddy.

'I want to lick every inch of your body,' he breathed, pulling his mouth away from hers. He pushed his tongue into the inner whorls of her ear as his fingers pressed up into her sex. The double assault produced a surge of feeling that made her moan.

His mouth moved to her shoulder. He pulled

131

the shoulder-strap of the teddy down her arm as he kissed and nibbled the soft skin, then helped her extract her arm from it. He licked at the tightly corded sinews at her throat. His mouth was hot and wet and Kate's body shuddered.

He pulled the other shoulder-strap down, and worked her arm out of it. She was lying flat on the bed and he was posed above her. His hand moved to the front of the teddy and began pulling the lacy bodice down slowly, so slowly she had the impression he was teasing himself, his eyes were riveted on her breasts.

'Beautiful,' he said, very quietly, as they were finally revealed.

The white silk caressed her flesh. She felt it slip over her left nipple and saw him staring at it.

'How yummy,' he whispered, then leaned forward and smothered her breast in little pecking kisses. After he'd covered the whole expanse he concentrated on the nipple, sucking it up into his mouth so hard that the surrounding flesh was drawn up too. He pulled his head back so her breast was stretched upward into a taut pyramid of flesh and she felt a sharp surge of pleasure.

He moved over to her right breast and followed exactly the same procedure, his lips kissing every inch of her flesh until he finally drew her nipple into his mouth and pulled back. At the same time the fingers of his left hand sank into her left breast, kneading it softly while his right continued to press into her sex, the silk crotch buried between her labia.

132

Kate's body trembled. She felt her clitoris throbbing and her sex clench. If she had had any misgivings about getting herself into this situation, they had gone, evaporated in the heat of the moment.

Peter was tugging the garment down over her waist. He kissed and licked and sucked at every inch of flesh he revealed. When the tight white silk got to her hips, she raised her buttocks off the bed and allowed him to strip the teddy down over her belly and her thighs. The crotch had become so embedded in her sex, it had to be tugged free.

He kissed her belly and her pubic hair, then moved down to her thighs. As his hands manoeuvred the teddy down to her knees, his mouth followed, licking the white lace stocking-tops and then the nylon, all the way down to her ankles, where he finally stripped the garment away. He pulled her shoes off and kissed her feet, then sucked on her toes, producing another surge of pleasure.

Kate looked up to see what he was doing. He knelt at her side, his erection sticking up from his thighs. It had produced its own lubrication which was smeared on his belly, making a little wet trail in the fine hair that grew there. He had her toes buried in his mouth. The extraordinary thing was that there seemed to be a secret conduit between the nerves there and the nerves in her sex that electrified both.

He moved his mouth back to her ankle, sucking at her flesh through the nylon. She saw his eyes staring at her naked sex. He worked up to her

133

knee, then pushed her legs apart and knelt between them, his eyes rooted to the apex of her thighs.

'What a lucky boy!'

The voice startled Kate momentarily. She had been so involved in her own feelings that she had forgotten about Marianne. She turned her head and saw her sitting on a little pink boudoir chair at the foot of the bed. She had her legs crossed and the fingers of her left hand were tucked under her right armpit, her forearm covering her breasts.

For a second, the two women's eyes met. Kate felt a surge of excitement. If she had any doubts that Marianne's presence would put a dampener on her arousal, they were instantly banished. The expression on Marianne's face gave nothing away, however; if the spectacle was exciting her, it did not show. Her eyes moved down Kate's naked breasts, then to the long expanse of slender thigh, banded by the broad lacy welt, with an almost indifferent gaze.

Peter had worked up to her thigh. Kate felt his mouth cross from white lace to naked flesh. He was so close to her sex she could feel his breath on it.

'So soft,' he said. 'Like the silk.'

She eased her legs further apart and felt her labia opening. She was wet. She could actually feel her juices running down her vagina and she was sure her whole vulva was glistening.

He moved his mouth onto her other leg, starting at the knee again and working up. Meanwhile his right hand slid over her belly and onto her pubic hair. He stroked it as if stroking a cat, smoothing her hair back against her body.

His lips sucked at her flesh. He was above the stocking-top again and rapidly approaching her sex. His lips kissed the sinews that stretched between from the top of her thigh to the base of her groin, then travelled up to the crease of her pelvis. They explored a few inches up this valley then dipped down again, over her delta and up on the other side, teasing her by studiously ignoring her pussy.

Impatient for contact, Kate pushed her hips up off the bed. Instantly, he moved his mouth down between her legs and kissed her labia, darting his tongue out between them. Kate moaned loudly. She felt his tongue push up towards her clitoris then, finding it hard and swollen, nudged it from side to side, producing a whole new series of sensations. At the same time, his fingers worked their way under her thigh. They found the cleft of her vagina and thrust inside. She had noticed how long his fingers were; they went deep, the silky walls of her sex parting to admit them.

She surrendered to pleasure; her eyes closed as waves of feeling engulfed her. She seemed to be able to feel the rough surface of his tongue as it rubbed across her clitoris. His mouth had set her whole body alight. Everywhere it had gone it had sensitised her flesh, its path marked out in criss-crossed lines of sensation, etching new erogenous zones all over her body, each responding with renewed vigour as her clitoris throbbed with stronger and stronger feeling.

She was coming. His touch was perfect. Her pleasure came in waves, a peak followed by a trough, and the tempo he used as his tongue pushed her little knot of nerves from one side over to the other corresponded to it exactly. His long fingers weren't pumping into her but were scissored apart, stretching the silky wet flesh of her vagina and creating another area of hot delight.

Kate felt all these different sensations coalesce, joining to form one, an entity much larger than its individual parts. But it was not only the physical pleasure that was turning her on. The fact that she knew Marianne was watching all this, her blue eyes staring at Kate's naked body stretched out on the bed, gave her feelings an extreme dimension, making them sharper and more piquant.

She fought to open her eyes, wanting to see Marianne again, but it was too late. Her orgasm swept up from her clitoris, wiping away the ability to do anything but feel. Every nerve in her body clenched, registering the shock of it, then wallowed in wave after wave of overwhelming delight that seemed to be endless.

It did end, of course, and Kate opened her eyes. Marianne was still sitting in the chair, but the dispassionate gaze had disappeared from her face replaced by a rather glazed look, her mind turned inward. She had uncrossed her legs and her fingers were hooked around the crotch of the black satin body, pulling it aside. Kate could see the lips of her sex and thought she glimpsed something embedded in Marianne's vagina.

Before she could focus on it, Peter's face loomed into view, hauling his body on top of hers. He kissed her on the mouth, his tongue pushing between her lips as he bucked his hips and plunged his cock into her open and soaking wet vagina. All thoughts of Marianne were lost as Kate felt herself impaled on his hard sword of flesh. Immediately her sex clenched convulsively around it, all the lush, extravagant feelings of orgasm that had just leached away instantly renewed, her need – or so it seemed – even greater than it had been before.

'Lovely,' he whispered in her ear. 'So silky . . .'

He began moving inside her, not at all gently. He pushed his cock right up into her, then pulled it almost all the way out, as his right hand groped for her breast. As he pounded into her, his fingers pinched at her puckered nipple.

'Can you come again?' he hissed.

'Yes.'

He really didn't have to ask. Her whole body was alive, stretched out beneath him on some imaginary rack, her nerves already in spasm. Each inward stroke caused paroxysms of pleasure. In seconds, she felt her clitoris jerking violently. She lifted her thighs, pulling them back towards her body, bending her knees, his cock slipping even deeper as her sex was angled up to meet his thrusts.

'Oh, God . . .' She threw her head to one side and

felt her orgasm explode. It was as though everything that had gone before was just a precursor to this, the power of sensation she felt this time so concentrated it made her scream. Her whole universe, every nerve, every feeling was narrowed down to the spot where the crown of his cock battered into the neck of her womb.

But the feelings did not ebb away, nor did he stop to let them. He hammered on, bucking his hips, forcing his cock forward, the silky wetness of her vagina a provocation to both of them.

Kate wanted more. 'Turn over,' she said, lowering her legs. 'I want to be on top. I want to do it to you.'

Almost before she'd said it, she felt his hands pushing under her back and wrapping around her. Clutching her to him, he rolled himself over onto his back and took her with him. Kate found herself on top, though his cock was still deep inside her.

'Clever boy,' she said.

Carefully, not wanting him to escape for a moment, she pulled her legs up until she was straddling his hips. In this position, his penetration was even deeper, but this time she was in control. She could push herself down on him, spreading her legs wide apart to get every last inch of penetration.

'Is that what you wanted?' he asked.

'Yes. You've got a wonderful cock.'

She began riding him, bouncing up off the bed and feeling his erection pumping into her. She looked at his body, spread out under her. Each downward movement produced a little twitch in the muscles of his face.

What she wanted now was to give this man who had pleasured her so beautifully the same treatment. She wanted to feel him come, feel his ejaculation deep inside her. And, in her current state of arousal, that would also certainly mean she would come again, too. She ran her hand down to her belly and nudged a finger between her labia. Her clitoris twitched as her finger butted against it.

'Shall I do that for you?'

Again she had forgotten about Marianne. The chair was empty. Kate twisted around to look for her. She was standing behind them, her eyes staring at Kate's buttocks, watching the way her husband's cock disappeared between them. The blonde reached forward and laid her hand on Kate's shoulder.

The touch was electric. Marianne moved closer. Her hand slid down to the upper surface of Kate's breast.

'No,' Kate cried aloud. But her body felt otherwise. As Marianne's hand brushed against the stiffness of her nipple, a tremor of sensation rocked through her. Instantly, her clitoris spasmed against her finger and, as she slammed herself down on Peter's cock, an orgasm as sudden as any she'd ever experienced began breaking over her. It was just as concentrated and just as strong as the first two, but she knew it was not caused by Peter. She didn't want to think about the implications, but there was no denying that it was the touch of

Marianne's hand that had brought her off this time.

Peter moaned loudly. Kate opened her eyes. Marianne's fingers, her long fingernails varnished a scarlet red, were still digging into the flesh of her breast. But it was the blonde's other hand that had produced the moan. Kate felt her fingers cupping Peter's scrotum. As she squeezed it Peter's cock jerked against the slippery tube of flesh that sheathed it so tightly. A jet of semen flooded into her vagina. Another followed, and another; Kate felt each one. Marianne's fingers squeezed again, milking out every last drop.

Chapter Seven

'*I'M SORRY, I* overstepped the line.'

They were sitting downstairs again, glasses of red wine in front of them. Marianne had wrapped a white cotton robe over the black satin body. Peter was upstairs taking a shower.

'You don't have to apologise, Marianne. You really don't.' Kate had no idea how she felt about what had happened but she knew she wasn't angry at the blonde. Given the situation she had volunteered herself for, that would have been more than faintly ridiculous.

'I haven't done it before, Kate. Never. There was just something about you. I couldn't resist. If you want the truth, I was having great trouble not jumping all over you.'

Kate laughed to relieve the tension, then sipped her wine. 'And you haven't felt that way before?'

'No. Yes. No. I mean, some of the women have been very attractive. But it was easy not to get involved. But with you . . .'

'What?'

'You want the truth?'

'I think so.'

'There's something about you, Kate. Have you ever . . . Do you mind me asking? Have you ever been with a woman.'

'No.'

'Or thought about it? Fantasised about it?'

'You're the second person in a week who's asked me about my fantasies.'

'And?'

'I've never really got around to having sexual fantasies. And recently I've been so involved, I haven't needed to.'

'What did you think about when you masturbated?'

'I didn't much. Perhaps that's why I was never very good at it.'

'You never imagined what it would be like to be touched by a woman?'

'No . . .' Kate hesitated.

'Why do you say it like that?'

'I had a letter from a woman. A lesbian. I thought about her a couple of times.'

'What sort of thoughts?'

'I'm not sure. It wasn't really sexual. I mean, I didn't imagine her standing by my bed with a dildo strapped around her body.'

'But the letter excited you?'

Kate thought for a moment. She couldn't separate the thoughts she'd had about the long-haired brunette from the sexual context that had surrounded them at the time. Thoughts of the brunette's quizzical eyes had provoked a sexual response, but only in a situation where she had been completely immersed in sex. 'Perhaps interest would be a better word. Can I ask you something, since we seem to be on the subject?'

'Anything.'

'What have you got on under that body?'

It was Marianne's turn to laugh. 'You spotted that, did you? My little friends.'

'Friends?'

'Front and back. To keep each other company.'

'Dildos?'

'Small and discreet. Peter usually sucks them out of me one by one then puts himself in their place. A body's ideal for keeping them in securely; you need something nice and tight. I wear them during the day sometimes, if I'm really horny.'

Kate sipped the wine again. 'So what do you think I should do?' she asked. There was something about Marianne that made her feel able to bring her feelings out into the open.

'About what?'

'About what you made me feel.'

'What I made you feel? I'm sorry, I'm lost.'

'When you touched me. You know you made me come.'

'Did I? I thought that was my husband.'

'No. It was you.' Kate could not suppress a shudder as she thought about it.

'Don't worry about it. Have a good night's sleep. You'll have forgotten about it in the morning. You were very turned on. It was probably just

143

the last straw that broke the camel's back.'

That was true, Kate thought. She *had* been very aroused. She was probably just letting her imagination run away with her.

'I'd better be going,' she said. 'Thanks.'

'You made the right decision, Kate. It was great.'

Kate stood up. 'What are you going to do now?'

Marianne smiled broadly. 'Do you have to ask?' She ran her hand down the front of her navel and pressed her fingers against her mons.

They walked to the front door together. As Marianne opened it, Peter appeared at the top of the stairs. He was wearing a small towel knotted around his waist.

'Bye, Kate. It was fun. I hope we'll see you again.'

'Bye.'

Peter disappeared back into the bedroom.

'I hope you are going to visit us again,' Marianne said.

'I will.'

'Is that a promise?'

'Promise.' Rather selfconsciously Kate leant forward and kissed Marianne on the cheek.

As she walked down the garden path, she heard the front door close. She imagined Marianne walking straight upstairs and into the bedroom. Peter would be laying naked on the bed. Marianne would kneel on the bed beside him, straddle his shoulders then undo the fastenings that held the gusset of the black satin body in place. She would ease herself forward, pushing her sex down to his mouth . . .

With a determined effort, Kate shut the thoughts out of her mind, closed the garden gate and set off to find her car.

'So what did you do?'

'I agreed, naturally.'

'Sarah! How do you get yourself into these situations?'

'Just a natural talent.'

Kate was sitting on the small terrace of Sarah Appleby's flat on the south side of the river in Battersea. The view of Chelsea Harbour and the setting sun was quite breathtaking.

'More champagne?'

'Not on an empty stomach.'

'Food will be ready, soon. It's only *boeuf bourguignon* and salad.'

'Sounds great.'

Sarah was Kate's oldest friend. They had known each other since they had both taken a law degree at college. Unfortunately, lately they seemed to be seeing less and less of each other. Sarah had given up the law after getting married. The marriage hadn't lasted long but the divorce settlement had left her so comfortably off – the flat and a Mercedes in the garage below all part of the deal – that she probably didn't have to work again.

'So what happened, then?'

Kate had decided she needed to talk to someone. She'd called Sarah, who'd invited her for dinner on Saturday night. Installed on the terrace

145

in temperatures that had made it the hottest day of the year so far, with a pleasant breeze drifting off the Thames, Sarah was busy telling her about a man at a party last week. He'd invited her out to an expensive dinner and then asked her if she'd come back to his flat. After he'd plied her with booze he asked her if she'd go to bed with him for money. Quite a lot of money. Five hundred pounds.

'The thing was, I'd have done it for nothing. He was dishy.'

'And?'

'He gave me the money in fifty-pound notes, just like that. He showed me the bedroom and asked me to take my clothes off. He wanted me to wear a pair of stockings and a suspender belt. They were brand new, still in their wrapping paper. He must have gone out and bought them specially. I didn't mind that – a lot of men are really into stockings. Anyway he went off to the bathroom and I got my gear off and put on these togs. I left my high heels on, too.'

'And?'

'Well, there's no accounting for taste. He walked in with one of those shiny black PVC macs. Wanted me to put that on too. So, I thought, to hell with it, in for a penny in for a pound. I put it on. He was wearing this little towel; the moment I put the mac on, his cock stuck up like the Eiffel Tower. I told him he had to wear a condom. When he put it on, he just walked up behind me, put his arms around me, felt my tits through the mac and made

146

this funny little coughing sound. Next thing I knew, he was running for the bathroom. It was seconds, less than seconds. Jesus. There are some funny people in this world.'

'What are you going to spend the money on?'

'A new mac.'

They laughed. Sarah excused herself to go and look at the food. The terrace was large enough for two comfortable wicker armchairs and a small circular dining table, which Sarah had laid with a gingham cloth. Sarah was no great beauty. She was rather plump and short with a round, jowly face and blonde hair that was permed into tight curls, but she had so much energy and life that she had no difficulty in attracting an endless stream of men.

A few minutes later, Sarah came back with a tray of food: a casserole dish, a basket of bread, a large bowl filled with green salad, and a bottle of red wine.

'So what have you been up to? I must say, I've never seen you looking so good.'

'Oh, this and that.' Having got herself invited to dinner to talk about what had happened to her over the last couple of weeks, now Kate wasn't at all sure what she wanted to say.

'A new man?' Sarah assumed men were the root cause of all female good health, or the lack of it.

'Several.' That was the truth, at least.

'Several? Doesn't sound like you.'

'I've decided work isn't everything.'

'What is this, friendship or sex?'

'Sex.'

'I never thought I'd live to hear you say that, Kate. I thought you were into serious, meaningful relationships.'

'That's the trouble. I was.'

'And now?'

'Now I've found sex has its compensations.'

'Anyone in particular?'

'It started with a barrister I knew, a couple of weeks ago.'

'That recent?'

Sarah opened the casserole. The aroma of beef and wine and herbs smelt delicious. She ladled it onto two plates and handed one across the table to Kate.

'Yes. He was the usual lying toad. He invited me out to dinner then back to his place. He must have caught me on the right night, or something, but he charmed me out of my knickers. Before I knew it, I was in bed with him.'

'Not Kate Hailstone – I don't believe it.'

'And he was good. Really good. The best I'd ever had. In fact, he made the others look like amateurs.'

'There has to be a but.'

'Exactly. Turned out he was married and we were doing it in the marital bed.'

'Bastard,' Sarah said, grinning. 'You are a prude, Kate.'

'It's not that. I don't like liars. But I have to say, I'm grateful to him. It made me realise—'

'That there's a whole new world out there, waiting for sexually emancipated women. So you went in search of Mr Right.'

'I went in search of a good screw.'

'God, Kate, I'm shocked.' Sarah mimed the emotion. 'And did you find it?'

'Yes.' She ate some of the stew. 'This is delicious.'

'And who was he?'

'I don't even know his second name.' That was the truth, too.

'And?'

'And what?'

'There's more. You said several, remember.'

'Have you ever seen the *City Times*?'

'You didn't!'

'Didn't what?'

'Take an ad in 'Kindred Spirits'? Christ, Kate, I'd never have believed it of you. So what happened? Tell me all. This is really good stuff. Did you get lots of replies? What did they send you, pictures of their dicks and tell you what they were going to do to you?'

'Some of them.'

'So what happened? Did you go on a wild rampage?'

Kate smiled. Sarah hadn't changed. Her attitude to life was refreshingly uncomplicated. She had never seen any reason not to take whatever opportunities for enjoyment, fun and pleasure that presented themselves and had never given a damn about the consequences.

'Not exactly.'

149

'Oh, come on. Give me the gory details. There must have been some.'

'Can I ask you something really personal, Sarah?' Kate sipped her wine and looked across the table at her friend. The sun had set and the light was suffused with a deep orange that lit up the chubby cheeks of Sarah's face, her broad smile creating two deep dimples. 'You don't have to answer.'

'Go on.' She sipped her wine and tore off a piece of bread, dipping it into the stew and mopping up the juices.

'Have you ever ... Have you ever made ... I mean, been with ... you know ... made love with a woman?'

Sarah laughed. 'Is that all? Christ, Kate, I thought you knew. Don't you remember Penny – that redhead who was always hanging around me in the junior common room? Didn't you realise she was a dyke? She was desperate to get into my knickers.'

'And you let her?'

'Eventually. Actually, it was fun. She was really good at it.'

'And since?'

'You know me, Kate, never one to let a good thing pass me by. Don't get me wrong, I don't go looking for it. But if I get an offer, I usually make myself available. Do you remember Derrick?'

'Your boss at Campion Drew?'

'Yes. Well, his wife was Italian. Real class. I think she was a countess or something. The last

Christmas party before I left, she made a beeline for me. She was all Valentino dresses, Joy perfume and silk lingerie – but for some reason she'd got the hots for little porky old me. She manoeuvred me into the stationery cupboard and was all over me like a rash.'

'Really?'

'Then Gabriella kept calling me. They had this house in Highgate. After the divorce, I decided I needed some light entertainment, so I accepted her invitation. I spent the afternoon with her.'

'You never told me.'

'I thought you'd be shocked.'

'And you did . . . I mean you . . .'

'I think we did everything two women can do to each other, yes. It was great. Sex is sex, as far as I'm concerned. Life's too short to worry about what gives you pleasure. It hasn't made any difference to my life. It hasn't put me off men; it just seems to increase my general all-round randiness. And it's terribly convenient. If I can't find a nice guy to do the business, then there's always a woman. It's much easier to take the initiative with a woman.'

'Do you still see Gabriella?'

'Occasionally, when I'm in the mood for a bit of luxury. They've got silk sheets.'

Kate ate her food determinedly. She finished the meat and used her bread to wipe the plate clean.

'So now it's your turn,' Sarah said. 'Why all this interest in my sex life?'

Kate looked at her friend. Their eyes met and she felt the same bond of affection the girl had

151

always inspired in her. 'Because I don't know what to do.'

'Some dyke's trying to coax you out of your knickers?'

'Not exactly.' And then it all came tumbling out and Sarah sat open mouthed as Kate, the friend she had regarded as staid and sensible, told her of her encounter with Marianne and Peter and the feelings it had aroused in her. She even mentioned the letter from the long-haired brunette and how she kept seeing the expression in the woman's eyes.

'Well you have gone for it, haven't you?' Sarah said. She shunted the stew plates aside and served the salad. 'Help yourself to cheese.'

'But I don't know what to do. It scares me.'

Sarah grinned. She had set two large candles on the table and got up to get matches to light them. They flickered in the cooling breeze from the river. A large barge went by, towing two others. 'Who was it who said you only ask advice from people who you know will tell you the advice you want to hear? You know what I'm going to say, Kate. It's obvious. If it feels right, go with it. If it doesn't, forget it. You wouldn't have come here if you thought I was going to tell you it was wicked and sinful.'

'I didn't know you were into women.'

'That doesn't matter. You know what my attitude is. *Carpe diem.*'

'Gather ye rosebuds while ye may . . .'

Sarah was right, of course. If Kate had told this story to Patsy Palmer – her other university friend, who was married with three children and a fourth on the way, and lived in deepest Somerset with her farmer husband – Patsy would have undoubtedly been shocked and told her she was making a grave mistake. She had come to Sarah because she knew Sarah would encourage and not be judgemental. She had come to Sarah so she would tell her what she wanted to hear.

'All right,' she said, cutting pieces from three cheeses. 'Since we're into true confessions, tell me more about Gabriella.'

Sarah leant back in the chair. 'What do you want to know?'

'Kate, I've got Mr Smythe on the phone for you,' Sharon said when Kate answered the phone.

'What does he want?'

'Your body?'

'He can join the queue. Put him through.'

'Kate, how are you?'

'Blooming. And you, Jonathan?'

'Well, thank you. The reason I'm calling is I've had an offer from the other side.'

'Really? I thought they were going to fight it all the way.'

'It's a rather good one actually. I have to tell you, Michael Arnold said he was very impressed with the work you'd put in. Between you and me, that's what swung it, I think. You'd covered all the bases in your brief. It was clear they had nowhere to go.'

'So what's the offer?'

'Two million and costs to date.'

'My God.'

'I'm sure your client will want to accept.'

'That's practically the whole claim. I doubt we'd have got that much in court.'

'Precisely. I'm going out to buy a bottle of champagne. I don't suppose you'd care to join me for dinner?'

'No, Jonathan, thank you,' she said firmly.

'Well, congratulations. I hope we can work together again.'

Kate put the phone down. She asked Sharon to get James Alexander Harding on the phone and told him the good news. His formal acceptance was faxed to Smythe who would complete the formalities with the other side's barrister.

The win was as unexpected as it was welcome. It would considerably boost her contribution to the partner's income and was yet another feather in her cap. It was very much a cause for celebration, the second in a week. As with the first she felt her elation had the effect of wiping out any lingering anxieties.

She had had the letter in her briefcase for two days. She'd taken it out a dozen times and put it back again. She picked up the phone. 'Sharon, five minutes DNB.' She didn't want Sharon bursting in during the middle of the call.

She opened her briefcase and took out the letter, then picked up the phone and punched in the number. It was a mobile phone.

'Hello?' The connection sounded distant.

'Oh, is that Pamela?'

'Yes.' The connection improved. 'Hold on, let me pull over.'

Kate thought she heard the noise of a car engine. After a second or two it stopped. 'Right, that's better. Who's calling?' The woman was American.

'Box 43.'

'Hi, Box 43. Jesus, I'd given up on you. It's great to hear your voice. What's your name?'

'Kate.'

'Nice. Classy.'

'I wondered if you'd like to meet up.'

'Hey, that would be real interesting. I'm on my way up to Leeds at the moment, but I'm back tomorrow.'

'Tomorrow's fine. Shall we meet for a drink somewhere?'

'Sure thing. My apartment's being done over at the moment. Stripped and completely remodelled, so I had to move out. I've got a room at the Carlton Hotel on Park Lane. Do you know it?'

'Yes.'

'What about in the bar downstairs at eight?'

'That sounds fine.'

'You've got the photograph, haven't you? So you'll recognise me.'

'Yes.'

'Great. See you, honey.'

Kate hung up. She felt short of breath and realised that, despite the office's air conditioning, a line of sweat had broken out on her upper lip.

*

155

It was getting hotter. The television news carried stories of record-breaking temperatures and dire warnings about global warming and drought. Water companies issued hose-pipe bans across most of southern England.

It was too hot to sleep. Or perhaps it was just that Kate had too much on her mind. She had gone to bed early, as her bedroom was the coolest room in the house, and tried to read but found her eyes were too tired. Despite that, sleep didn't come once she'd put the book down.

She lay thinking about tomorrow night.

Pamela had sounded relaxed and confident. Kate imagined her sitting in the bar of the hotel, her expression the same as the one in the photograph, her legs crossed and her eyes somehow looking at Kate and through her at the same time.

It was difficult to forget what had happened with Marianne. She had been prepared to accept that in the midst of the excitement she had been experiencing, Marianne's touch meant nothing. But as time had passed, she became increasingly convinced that wasn't true.

Whatever had happened to her recently, the sexual feelings that Duncan had released refused to be satisfied. He had woken a sleeping giant, who was now determined to lumber through Kate's life.

What Sarah had said was reassuring. If she had ever thought about lesbians, Kate supposed she had an image of women in men's suits, with slicked-back hair and strapped-down bosoms. She didn't want that. But the thought of Gabriella – whom she remembered as one of the most elegant and sophisticated women she had ever seen – and Sarah in bed together was much more acceptable.

Kate threw the single sheet that covered her body to one side. She was naked. There must have been a bright moon as there was enough light spilling in through the gaps in the curtains for her to see her body. She looked down at it: the weight of her breasts pulled them to one side and the flatness of her navel led to the perpendicular stripe of pubic hair, and below that her long slender legs. She felt little rills of sensation stirring in her sex. As she watched, she saw her nipples stiffen.

Casually, she cupped her left breast in her hand, pushing the flesh back up onto her chest. Its nipple pulsed. Without the desire to do anything but satisfy her curiosity, she tweaked the same nipple between her thumb and forefinger. It pulsed more strongly, making the other nipple respond too.

Kate remembered the way Peter had licked and sucked her body from head to foot and the effect it had had on her. She moved her other hand to her right breast and held that one firmly too, then moved her fingers to both nipples and tweaked them simultaneously. The resultant surge of feeling made her moan.

She raised her head and looked at the small sofa. She imagined Marianne sitting there. She could see the way the black satin clung to the curves of her body, her small breasts outlined under it and the look in her eyes, cool and uninvolved. She remembered how the blonde had held the crotch of the body aside and she'd glimpsed what she now knew was the stub of a dildo buried in her vagina.

Still kidding herself that it was just a matter of casually exploring her body, Kate let her right hand travel down to her belly. Her pubic hair felt as if it were charged with static electric, brittle and tingling. She brushed it gently then sent her hand lower, down between her legs.

'No,' she said aloud, pulling her hand away.

She lay still, both hands at her sides, and closed her eyes tight. But it was too late. Her body was alive with little thrills and pulses of feeling that refused to die away.

Annoyed with herself for starting something she didn't really want to finish, she rolled onto her stomach and opened the middle drawer of the left-hand bedside chest. It was where she kept her silk scarves. She picked out the first one that came to hand. Sitting up, she folded the scarve into a neat strip and wrapped it around her eyes, knotting it so tightly that it pressed against her eyeballs. The feeling made her sex pulse.

She groped around in the darkness and opened the top drawer of the chest. Her fingers settled on the unmistakable shape of the vibrator. She took it out.

Kate lay back on the bed. Her whole body was rippling with feeling, her nipples as hard as pebbles. She squeezed her thighs together and felt a wetness seeping out over her labia.

In the blank screen of her mind, behind the blindfold, images flickered and danced. She saw Peter lying on the double bed and Gerard wrapping the black silk over her eyes. She saw Tom's erection forcing its way into her body. But then her mind seemed to focus on Pamela, her face staring out from the colour photograph, those eyes watching her every movement.

Kate grasped the dildo firmly in her right hand and opened her legs, bending them at the knee. She turned the gnarled knob at the base of the shaft and heard a loud hum. The vibration affected her hand and much of her lower arm. Slowly, she ran the tip of the dildo up her thigh and nosed it between her labia. She let out a little yelp of delight as the vibrations seized her clitoris.

Pamela sat on the sofa at the foot of the bed. She was wearing the same black satin body that Marianne had worn and the same hold-up stockings. Her long hair was brushed out over her shoulders. She was smiling but it was a thin critical smile, her eyes staring at Kate's sex.

'Is this what you want to see?' Kate said aloud, her body throbbing with arousal now. She arched her buttocks off the bed and moved the dildo down until it was parting the lips of her vagina. Her other hand clutched at her left breast, squeezing the flesh so hard she produced a spasm of pain. The pain, as she had known it would, turned to pleasure, the super-heated pleasure she'd felt before.

There was no pretence now. Her whole body

was geared up for orgasm, her need coursing through every nerve. But she held the dildo steady, teasing herself, making herself wait.

She opened her eyes but could see nothing. For a moment she thought of Gerard. She felt the hot, hard phallus pressing up into her rear passage. Her sex clenched, as if trying to suck the dildo deeper.

Pamela got to her feet. She was tall. She put one foot up on the end of the bed and began to roll down her stockings. She pulled them off each foot and dropped them onto the floor. They floated down like feathers. Bending over, the brunette released the crotch of the body. Kate strained to see more. Her sex was covered in a mat of black pubic hair.

'Oh, God . . .' A sharp pang of pure pleasure made Kate's body shudder. Releasing her breast, she moved her hand down to her clitoris. As lightly as she could, she touched the tip of her finger against the little bud of nerves, producing a surge of feeling. Her sex clenched again, as strongly as a fist, demanding attention. It was wet. She could feel little riverlets of moisture trickling down inside her.

She imagined Pamela kneeling on the bed beside her, dipping her head down so her mouth was poised above her breast, her tongue extended an inch from her nipple. She watched the brunette's hand hover above her belly.

'No,' she cried aloud.

But the hand did not stop. It brushed against her

160

pubic hair then curved down, cupping itself around the pubic bone.

'Oh, God.' Kate skittered her fingers across her clitoris. It responded with a whole symphony of feelings that wound her need higher. She could feel the mouth of her sex opening and closing convulsively but still she held the vibrator steady, letting the vibrations play through the whole crease of her vulva.

'Please,' she said aloud.

The feelings were mounting, her whole body stretched out and needy, her mind charged up too, her imagination running riot. Every nerve was screwed to fever pitch, her orgasm approaching rapidly now, inspired just as much by visions of Pamela as it was by the physical provocations.

Her hand was moving so fast it was almost a blur. Under this double assault, the lateral movement of her fingers and the strong waves of vibration from the dildo, her clitoris twitched massively. Kate's head arched backward, her throat at the same height as her chin. The vibrations were extending out to her anus too, making her sphincter pucker.

'Please,' she begged the anonymous person who controlled her hand. But she knew what she wanted. She wanted to be teased and tormented. Somewhere in a part of her mind which was still capable of rational thought, she wondered how she had managed to live so much of her life completely insensible to the extraordinary feelings she was experiencing now.

Ultimately, her body could stand no more. Like an elastic band pulled too tight, it snapped. She felt her orgasm rushing out from her clitoris and, in the last millisecond before it took total control, jammed the vibrating dildo deep into her sex, pushing it so far up that the stub end almost disappeared. She scissored her legs together to hold it in place as its penetration produced a second wave of pleasure as intense as the first. Her orgasm bubbled and boiled through her body, feelings so profound that she found herself making little moaning sounds long after the major impact had finally faded away.

She turned over onto her back and allowed her legs to open. She felt the vibrator slide slowly out of her sex. As it dropped onto the bed, she felt a final throes of pleasure, then rolled onto her side and curled into a ball. In seconds she was fast asleep.

Chapter Eight

THE BAR OF the Carlton Hotel was glitzy and modern. It had a black carpet and black cube-shaped leather and chrome armchairs, with square glass tables between them. The bar itself was a long structure in an S-shaped curve made from stainless steel with chrome bar stools all along its length.

'Can I help you, madam?' A tail-coated *maître d'* had come up to Kate as she entered the bar.

'I'm waiting for one of your guests.'

'Certainly, madam. Would you prefer a table or the bar?'

'A table, please.'

'Follow me.' He led her across the large room to a corner table. Across the room a jazz trio played *Misty*.

'May I get you a drink?'

'A glass of champagne.'

'Certainly, madam.' He walked away.

Kate looked round. The bar was busy, most of the tables inhabited by parties of men but with a

163

few women dotted among them. The walls of the room were cleverly inset with mirrors so reflections of reflections caught the eye.

A waiter in a white linen jacket and gold epaulettes brought a tall champagne flute, frosted with condensation. He set it down on a little paper coaster bearing the hotel's logo, then placed a little silver bowl of pistachio nuts beside it.

'Thank you,' Kate said.

'My pleasure, madam,' he said.

She watched as he returned to the bar. It was ten minutes to eight. Kate had wanted to make sure she was early. She wanted to see Pamela first and watching her cross the room would give her that opportunity. If for some reason she did not like what she saw, if the photograph had been carefully arranged to portray a flattering angle, or if she just felt that the unconscious signals she generated were wrong, she would have some seconds to decide whether to raise her hand and attract the woman's attention or to leave it down, finish her champagne and walk out.

She sipped the champagne. To her left, two women talked earnestly in whispers, their heads almost touching. Both were wearing black suits and looked as if they had come straight from work.

Kate tried to relax. She stretched her neck as she realised the muscles in her shoulders were tense, and sat back in the chair, trying to give the appearance of being at ease. She was wearing a clinging red jersey dress she had bought two days ago. It had a plunging neckline and a mid-thigh length skirt and was probably the tartiest outfit she had ever bought for herself, but it seemed particularly appropriate for tonight. She hadn't the slightest idea what a woman would find attractive on another woman, but wearing this dress excited her, so logically it should have the same effect on Pamela.

Was that what she wanted? Was she really sitting in this bar waiting to meet a woman who wanted to take her to bed? If someone had told her three weeks ago that this is what she would end up doing, she would have thought they were mad.

Oddly, she didn't feel in the least bit nervous. The emotions she'd experienced as she'd walked up the path to Peter and Marianne's house were absent – all bar the excitement. And even that was different. It was an excitement buried under an analytic objectiveness. Kate's mind was leading this expedition into the unknown for once, not her body. At least, that's what she liked to think.

'Excuse me.'

She looked up. A man had crossed the room towards her. He was wearing a beautifully cut navy blue suit, a white silk shirt and a blue patterned silk tie. His highly polished black shoes looked as if they were hand-made.

'Yes?'

'Are you Anabelle Harmsworth?'

'No, I'm not,' Kate said calmly. The man had thick blond hair and ice cold blue eyes.

'Oh. What a pity. I was really hoping that you were,' he said.

'I'm sorry. There's nothing I can do about it.'

'No . . . Of course not.' He hesitated then half-turned away. 'Ah, I don't suppose . . .' He turned back towards her. 'I don't suppose you'd care to have a drink with me?'

'I'm waiting for someone. So are you.'

'Yes. I know . . . I just thought.'

'Another time, perhaps.'

'That would be nice. Here.' He took out his wallet, extracted a small white card and handed it to her.

'Thank you,' she said in a mocking tone.

'You know you're really gorgeous, don't you? Really.'

'Am I?'

He saw a reflection in one of the mirrors, smiled at her tamely and headed off towards the girl who had just come in. Kate watched him take her elbow and guide her to the bar. As she struggled onto the bar stool, her skirt rode up. The man stared at her shapely thighs.

She put the card down without looking at it. There was an electric clock on the wall, just two black hands mounted on a stainless steel circle with two black dots where the twelve and six would normally have been. It was eight o'clock.

Kate watched the entrance. Five minutes later, Pamela walked through the door. She was unmistakable, her long jet-black hair flowing out over her bare shoulders. She was wearing a tight black dress made entirely from lace and very sheer shiny black tights. The lace revealed the outline of a tiny

166

black satin bra and the even smaller triangle of the panties that covered her mons. She was wearing high-heeled ankle boots, the heels covered in shiny silver foil.

The American took three strides into the bar. The *maître d'* took three strides towards her. They surveyed the room together.

Without any hesitation, Kate raised her hand. 'Hi.'

Kate watched Pamela walk over to the table. Her body was slender and gave the impression of athleticism. She had long legs and was tall, with a narrow waist and a firm but not large bosom.

'Hello.' Pamela leant forward and kissed Kate on the cheek as if they were old friends. 'I never know whether it's *de rigueur* to give one kiss in Europe or two.' she asked, smiling. She had a large mouth with spectacularly white and regular teeth.

'In France, it's three.'

'Really?'

'May I get you a drink, madam?' The *maître d'* had followed her to the table.

'The same,' she said, indicating Kate's glass. 'And another for my friend.'

The *maître d'* nodded and walked back towards the bar.

'Listen, sorry I wasn't very chatty on the phone. I hate those mobile things, especially when I'm on the road. But I have to have one.'

'What do you do?'

'I buy fashion for Stricklands.'

'How interesting.' Stricklands was an expensive

167

but very fashionable chain of boutiques with branches in London, Rome, Paris and New York. Her job explained a lot about the clothes Pamela was wearing.

'What about you?'

'Solicitor.'

'Hey, high-powered stuff.'

The waiter arrived with the champagne.

'So, cheers,' Pamela said. They clinked glasses. 'I hope you didn't mind me writing. I don't do it a lot. There was just something about your ad that appealed to me – nice turn of phrase, "lover not friend". And I meant what I said. Sometimes it's not that a woman can't get off because she's with the wrong man, but because she's with a man and not a woman.'

'That's not my problem,' Kate said thoughtfully.

'Yeah? So why are you here?'

'Curiosity.'

Pamela grinned, showing her teeth again. 'Hey, you know what curiosity did.'

'What about you? Can I ask you the same question? Why are you here?'

She leant back in the chair. If Kate cared to look she could see the way her black satin panties folded into her sex. 'I'm a dyke, right. I'm not into men at all. Not at all. Apart from female digits, the only thing I've had up me is made from synthetic polymers. It may be cock-shaped but it sure in hell ain't a cock. I like females. But I'm very selective. I ain't into butch dykes with attitude. Nothing like that.' She leant forward and picked up her cham-

168

pagne glass. She had slender hands. Her finger-nails were varnished in a blue so deep it was almost black. Her eye make-up was dark blue too. 'What I do like, what I really like, is finding some-one who's not been there before. That's a turn-on for me.'

'So you write letters.'

'Like I say, only occasionally. Mostly it's friends of friends. You develop a sort of sixth sense with some women. You'd be surprised. I'm not saying there's a lot of dykes waiting to come out of the closet, but there's a whole bunch of women who have thought about it and don't mind, shall we say . . . drinking from the other side of the cup. Like you say, curiosity. Hey, listen you're a real looker. What's this?' She picked up the white card the man had left.

'A man tried to pick me up before you arrived.'

'Really? Jesus, nowhere's safe. Were you tempted?'

'No.'

'Do I take it this is your first time?'

'Yes.'

'So why now? I mean, why have you suddenly got curious?'

'Because I've suddenly got interested in sex I suppose.'

'And you're checking out all the angles?' She laughed.

'I suppose you could put it that way.' Kate liked the American. She seemed to have the same zest for life that made Sarah so special.

169

'OK, honey. I think you're great. Now, you've got two choices. One: we go and get a nice dinner in their not too sloppy restaurant, then say goodnight. Two: I take you up to my room and we get room service.'

For the first time that evening, Kate felt a pang of apprehension. 'I haven't done this before.'

'So you said. Listen, you want to go home and call me in a couple of days, that's no problem.'

Kate sipped at her champagne. Pamela crossed her legs. The American was looking at her in exactly the same way as she had looked in the photograph, one of her thick black eyebrows raised in a question.

'Room service, then,' she said, putting the champagne glass down.

They travelled up in the lift to the seventh floor with another couple who talked incessantly about the price of garden furniture. Pamela led the way down a long corridor carpeted in dark green Wilton. She took a card out of her small black handbag and inserted it into the lock mechanism. The door sprung open.

'*Chez moi*,' she said, standing back to allow Kate in first.

Kate found herself in a small hallway with a beige marble floor. A pair of double doors led into a large sitting room with spectacular views over Hyde Park. The room was luxurious. Obviously Stricklands paid their buyers well.

'What a view,' Kate said.

170

'Quite something, isn't it?'

Kate went over to the window and stared out. People were drifting out of the park though some were still lying on the grass or in deckchairs. Pamela came up to stand beside her.

'How long before your flat's ready?' Kate asked, suddenly feeling a little awkward. She supposed it was exactly like being with a man, those uncomfortable moments of adjustment between word and deed, between agreeing to go to bed and actually doing it.

'Oh, a month, I guess.'

'Where is it?'

'Grosvenor Square, just behind here.'

'Nice.'

'Hey, I know what you're thinking, no wonder Stricklands is so expensive, right? Ain't nothing to do with that. I'm a rich bitch. My daddy made a fortune dealing junk bonds, and he's a very generous man.'

'Really?'

Pamela put her hand on the nape of her neck. Her fingers felt cool and Kate's flesh puckered with goose-pimples. The hand ran all the way down her spine to the spherical curve of her buttocks. 'Nice ass,' she said casually. 'Here, let me give you the guided tour.'

Her hand dropped away. She led Kate across the room and back into the small hall. There was a door at the far end. 'Bedroom,' she said, opening it. This time she went first, leaving Kate to follow. 'And bathroom.' She was standing by a door to the

171

right of a large double bed indicating a white marble bathroom.

'Very nice,' Kate said. The bedroom was lush too, decked in flounced and frilled curtains, an equally elaborate counterpane and a canopy over the large double bed. A separate alcove held two banks of wardrobes, the doors painted in extravagant *faux* tortoiseshell which matched the bedside tables and a large chest of drawers.

Pamela smiled. She took two steps towards Kate and looked her straight in the eyes. 'This is the moment you turn and run,' she said.

Kate smiled, too. Her heart was beating like a drum, but she did not feel in the least like running away. She was here because she wanted to be here. She had not made the decision to call Pamela lightly. It had been the culmination of a number of things. In fact, though she was excited, the calmness and objectivity she had felt in the bar downstairs still prevailed. This was all by nature of an experiment.

She could see herself with Pamela in this luxurious bedroom as if from above, as though she were not there at all but merely observing what went on. 'I'm not going to do that.'

'Good.'

Eighteen inches separated them. Pamela took a step forward, covering the distance. She raised her hand and touched Kate's cheek, then very slowly leant forward until their lips were just brushing against each other's. Her hand moved round Kate's neck until it was at the back of her head and then she pulled Kate closer, their lips making firmer contact.

Wanting to take the initiative, Kate wrapped her arms around the girl and plunged her tongue into her mouth. She was astonished at how different it felt from kissing a man. Not only was Pamela's body soft and pliable in her arms, her mouth was much more malleable, moulding itself to her. Immediately she felt Pamela's tongue pushing hers back, the two dancing against each other, vying for position. As she pressed her body forward, she was intensely aware of the American's firm breasts pushing into her own. She could feel the girl's nipples like little pebbles buried in the mass of flesh, just as acutely as she could feel her own. But what struck her most, and excited her more than anything, was the fact that when she pushed her pelvis forward, there was no growing phallus pressing into her belly, only the flatness of Pamela's own navel and the hardness of her pubic bone.

Kate raised her thigh, pushing it up between Pamela's legs.

'Hey, slow down,' Pamela said. 'Let's take it nice and slow, baby.'

'I didn't think it would feel so different,' Kate said.

'Why don't we get a little bit more comfortable? Unzip me, will you, hon?'

Pamela turned her back on her. Kate found the tongue of the long zip on the lace dress and slid it down. The American pulled her arms out of the sleeves of the dress and let it fall to the floor. Her flesh was smooth and tanned. She reached behind her back and unclipped her bra, then tossed it aside. Without any selfconsciousness she turned to face Kate. Her breasts were small, but firm and round with wide bands of areola around each. The areola and her nipples were a dark reddish-brown, the nipples as large as cherries.

Kate couldn't remember the last time she had seen another woman's breasts. She'd never been into sports or health clubs, so had never come across women in the showers; nor did she go to the sort of shop with large open changing rooms.

Pamela put a foot up on the bed and unzipped the short fastening of her ankle boots, then kicked them off. Then she hooked her thumb into the waistband of the sheer black tights and pulled them down to her knees. Sitting on the edge of the bed, she stripped the nylon from her ankles, leaving her naked apart from the tiny triangular black panties.

'Your turn, hon,' she said, as she pulled the counterpane and the top bedding to the floor at the foot of the bed.

Kate gripped the hem of the jersey dress and wriggled it up over her hips. She got it to her waist then yanked it up over her head. She was wearing flesh-coloured tights, a pair of white jacquard panties and a matching underwired bra that fastened at the front. The jersey dress had been so tight the lines of the lingerie had been visible under it, but as Kate was aiming for obviousness that only served to emphasise the impression.

Pamela was lying in the middle of the bed.

'So what do you expect now, I wonder?' she said.

'Expect?' Kate said, taking off her high-heeled shoes.

'You want me to strap on a dildo and fuck you with it?'

Kate laughed. 'Is that what you usually do?' She sat on the edge of the bed and fumbled with the clip of the bra. It refused to come free.

'Let me,' Pamela said. She sat up and scrambled over to Kate. Her fingers hooked themselves under the front of the bra and prised the clasp open. Kate's heavy breasts fell out of the cups.

'Mmm, nice.' Pamela dipped her head and licked Kate's left breast, using the whole breadth of her tongue, like a child licking an ice-cream. As the rough surface of Pamela's tongue came into contact with the nipple Kate felt a sharp pang of pleasure.

The American got to her knees, pulled the bra off Kate's shoulders and threw it aside. Coming up behind Kate, she moved her hands around Kate's body and cupped both her breasts, squashing the soft flesh back against her ribs.

'Great tits,' she whispered. 'I'd kill for tits like these.'

The American's fingers found her nipples. She did not pinch them but rolled them between her fingers. Lowering her mouth to Kate's shoulder, she sucked on the bone then moved to the softer flesh of the neck.

Kate shuddered, her head forced back reflexively. The American's mouth worked up to her ear, her tongue burrowing into it. Then she kissed the back of it, right up to her hairline, her fingers still rolling both Kate's nipples like tiny wheels.

The sensations coalesced. Kate felt the now familiar pulses swirling through her body. She twisted around, tearing Pamela's hands from her breasts, pushed her back onto the bed, scrambled up on top of her and kissed her full on the mouth, plunging her tongue between her lips. She lay on top of her as she pushed their mouths together, writhing her body against her too, luxuriating in the softness and fluidity she had never encountered before. Their two bodies seemed to melt together, the line between them indistinct.

'I'm very turned on,' she said, without moving her lips away from Pamela's mouth.

'You sure are.' The American raised her leg, pushing it between Kate's thighs. She pressed it up until it was hard against Kate's labia and Kate felt her juices being smeared over Pamela's skin.

They kissed again, harder and longer, their bodies clinging to each other, Pamela's thigh flattened into Kate's groin. Their breasts swelled out at the side as they were squashed together, their nipples tingling with pleasure. Kate was astonished at how quickly her body had responded to this new experience. She had expected to find her physical responses muted and slow, while her mind coped with the minefield of taboo and

176

conventions that had to be set aside before she could fully enjoy herself. But it appeared that that was not a problem. The years of heterosexual conditioning had disappeared in seconds. In fact, she realised the very fact that she had thought of this as taboo and forbidden, as something beyond the pale, only twisted her excitement to a higher pitch.

Pamela lowered her leg and rolled Kate over onto her back. She pulled her mouth away from Kate's lips and immediately planted it on her left breast, hoovering her nipple up hungrily, while her hand closed on the right. She pinched both simultaneously, one with her teeth, one with her darkly varnished fingernails, causing a double twinge of pain followed, inevitably, by a twin thrill of prodigious pleasure.

The mouth moved lower. It left a wet trail on her flesh as the American licked her way downwards. As it approached her delta Kate felt her pulse racing. She levered her legs apart and arched her sex up almost imperceptibly.

Pamela's hands worked under Kate's thighs, then seized the gusset of the jacquard panties and pulled it aside. She raised her head and looked down at her labia. Gently, she used the tip of her fingers to draw the lips apart, exposing the scarlet slit of Kate's vagina and the little pink almond of her clitoris.

Kate moaned. She could feel Pamela's hot breath against her delicate flesh. She raised her head to look at the American, and felt a sharp throb of excitement as she saw her staring at her sex. She had never allowed a woman to see what the American could see now.

Then Pamela dipped her head forward. Kate saw her mouth open and her tongue dart out. It inched towards her clitoris. As Pamela's tongue touched it, a powerful surge of feeling jolted through her, like an electric shock, making her snap her head back and close her eyes. The secondary wave of feeling was almost as sharp as the first. She wasn't sure what the girl was doing to her but the feelings were so raw it was as if her tongue had somehow wriggled its way inside the little nut of nerves. Men had done this to her many times before, but it had never felt like this.

The objectivity, the spirit of intellectual discovery she had felt earlier, completely disappeared. In seconds, her whole body seemed to have closed around her clitoris, every feeling she had centred there. She had this odd sensation in her vagina – not clenching as it usually did, but doing the exact reverse, opening itself, the inner muscles becoming soft and relaxed. Instantly Kate felt her orgasm blossoming, a convulsion of pure pleasure that made her whole body quiver. She put her head back and uttered a long, low moan, a keening noise she did not recognise.

Pamela did not stop. Her tongue was not so much moving against Kate's clitoris as becoming part of it, wriggling and writhing to the rhythms of Kate's body. She did not circle it or nudge it from side to side but just held it pressed back against the pubic bone, somehow magnifying its own pulses. Almost instantly Kate came again, less sharply this time, a feeling like a wave of heat radiating through her body.

She struggled to regain some semblance of control. She raised her head. 'Now you,' she said breathlessly.

Pamela did not need to ask what this meant. She sat up and immediately pulled the tiny black satin panties down over her hips. She raised her buttocks and skinned them down her legs. Kate saw a thick mat of tight black curls covering her mons. She caught hold of the waistband of Kate's panties next and pulled those down too, dropping both pairs together on the sheet.

She looked at Kate's face. Her expression was no longer quizzical, as it had been earlier, but appeared totally involved, her eyes narrow and unblinking windows to a soul that was suffused with lust.

For a second she did nothing, building the tension between them. Then, with a glimmer of a smile flickering on her lips, she swung one leg over Kate's chest, straddling her breasts, her legs spread wide apart, her sex exposed.

Kate stared. For the first time in her life she found herself looking at another woman's sex. She had never really seen her own. Pamela was very hairy; her curly black hair ran down between her legs, thickly covering the wide bank of flesh on either side of her labia as well as the labia and extending right up to the little perfectly circular hole of her anus. Her labia themselves were thin but pursed like a mouth in anticipation of a kiss, the hair that covered them plastered back by her own juices.

Kate raised her hand. Very gently, as though she might damage it, she wrapped her fingers around the entire plane of the American's sex. The heat and wetness of it shocked her and she caught her breath. Tentatively she opened her fingers, dragging the labia apart, and found herself staring into the sticky scarlet flesh of Pamela's vagina.

Kate hooked her hands around Pamela's thighs and pulled her down towards her. The American lowered herself slowly. Impatiently Kate raised her head, planting her lips on Pamela's vulva and kissing it hard then squirming her tongue out between Pamela's labia. To her satisfaction, she felt Pamela's body tremble as the tip of her tongue nosed against the unmistakable protuberance of her clitoris.

Kate hadn't the faintest idea what to do. This was all totally new to her. Wanting to please Pamela as much as the American had already pleased her might not be easy, but she tried to remember what men had done to her in this position and what she had liked. Using this as a guide, she pressed the clitoris back against the underlying bone, then began to circle it with the tip of her tongue.

Pamela stretched forward. She could just reach the drawer of the bedside table. She opened it and extracted two small dildos. Laying them on the bed by Kate's thigh, she dropped forward and ran her hands under her thighs again, levering them apart. She pushed her head down and buried her tongue in Kate's labia for a second time.

Kate gasped. Suddenly everything changed. It was like completing a circuit, an electric current flowing through them both, charging everything up. Each action was matched by an exact and equal reaction. As Kate fought to concentrate on Pamela's pleasure, moving her tongue around her clitoris, she felt Pamela doing exactly the same thing to her. The fact that she could feel the effect it was having on the other woman as well as the effect it had on her seemed somehow to double the pleasure. Every tremble, every sensation was echoed from one to the other. But, unlike an echo, they did not fade away. Instead, the feelings grew, the resonances increasing.

It was as though there was no dividing line between their bodies, as if they had become one. For Kate tonguing Pamela's clitoris was almost like tonguing her own.

What was more, their orgasms were in tune too. As Kate's body screwed itself up to breaking point, she could feel Pamela's reacting in exactly the same way, each step closer registering on some invisible scale. Soon they were both at the brink, both gasping for oxygen, both totally concerned with the other's pleasure because through it they could achieve their own. If there was a millisecond's difference between the time when they finally lost control, and their orgasms broke like a violent storm, it was Pamela who came first. But even before Kate could register the enormous shudder of feeling that shook every part of the American's body, her own was suffering the same fate, the two women clinging to each other for support as they drowned in a turbulent sea of passion.

But that was not the end, only the beginning. Almost immediately, before the little tremors and thrills had completely died away, Kate felt a new element enter the equation. Something cold and hard was being thrust into her vagina. At the same time, she felt Pamela's hand groping backwards towards hers and pressing another object into it. It didn't take her long to realise what it was.

Then symmetry was restored. Kate brought the little dildo up to Pamela's sex and, while her tongue worked at Pamela's clitoris, she pushed the dildo into Pamela's sex, watching with fascination as the American's labia parted to admit it, pouting around it like a little mouth as it was thrust inside.

Pamela turned the vibrator's motor on. As a muffled hum filled the air and Kate felt her sex churning with vibrations, she found the control switch too and a second hum joined the first. Again, it was as though Kate could feel Pamela's reaction to the strong vibrations as acutely as she could feel her own. Again, both women's bodies appeared perfectly in synch. Again, Kate struggled to combat her own feelings, desperate to circle Pamela's clitoris with the same rhythm she was using to drive the little dildo in and out because that was exactly what Pamela was doing to her. And again their orgasms came, for all intents and purposes together, although this time it was probably Kate who was fractionally ahead.

Wave after wave of the most intense pleasure flooded through them both. It seemed to go on forever, like a storm trapped in the mountains, going round in circles, the gap between the thunder and the lightning never very great, the gap between the physical sensations and the feelings they produced so close as to be undetectable. Gradually, however, the storm ran its course, and feelings leached away.

Eventually, Pamela rolled onto her side. 'Are you all right?' she asked, twisting around and nuzzling her head against Kate's shoulder.

'I'm still trembling,' Kate said. She saw herself again, as if she were an observer of the event and not a participant, looking down at her body lying naked on the bed with another naked woman, their panties twisted together on the sheet at their feet, a pair of white dildoes in evidence too, their shafts glistening wet. Her body felt as if she had had an electric shock, trembling and numb at the same time. 'And something else,' she said.

'What?' the American asked.

'I'm starving.' She grinned.

Pamela sat up. She stretched over Kate's legs, her breasts brushing her calves, and managed to grab the phone.

'Room service, please,' she said. She put her hand over the receiver. 'So what exactly do you want?'

183

Chapter Nine

'*I HAVE TO* see you.'

'When?'

'Now.'

'It's midnight.'

'Does that matter? You're still on Australian time, aren't you?'

'OK.'

'What's the address?'

'Oh, right. I forgot you've never been here. Flat 4, Harlow Place, Ladbroke Grove. The Notting Hill end.'

'I know it.'

Without another word, she pressed the 'end' button on the carphone and drove off, thanking the God she didn't believe in that Notting Hill gate was so close. There was traffic around Hyde Park Corner but the Bayswater Road was clear and she accelerated well above the legal limit.

It took her eight minutes. She was lucky to find a parking space in Ladbroke Grove itself and ran to the modern block of flats identified as Harlow

Court by letters carved in the concrete wall that surrounded it.

She rang the bell on the entryphone. Almost immediately, the door lock buzzed and she pushed the door open. Number 4 was on the ground floor at the back. She ran along the corridor towards it and hammered on the door.

'Hi.' Tom was wearing a black cotton kimono.

Kate clasped his face in her hands and kissed him full on the mouth, thrusting her tongue between his lips. She pushed him back into his hallway and slammed the door closed with her foot. Pressing forward, she trapped him against the hall wall, grinding her body against his just as she crushed their mouths together.

'What's got into you?' he said.

'For Christ's sake, Tom, you've got to fuck me,' she said, before she covered his mouth with hers again, writhing her body from side to side. She ran her hand down his body and found his wrist, grabbing it and pushing it down between their bellies and up under the jersey dress. Her sex was like molten lava, hot and meltingly soft.

'You've got to fuck me, Tom. Please.' She had never wanted a man more in her life. Never. It had begun just after she had left Pamela. They had dined on club sandwiches and red wine, then fallen back onto the bed and repeated everything they had done before, with as much passion and desire. But as they had kissed goodbye and Kate had got in the lift, she had felt the one need that Pamela could not satisfy. After the softness of a woman, she needed the hardness and power of a man.

Tom was the only choice. She didn't want the complexity of Gerard or the complications of calling Peter and Marianne; and she certainly had no intention of calling Duncan, even if his wife was away. Fortunately Tom had got back from Australia on Tuesday.

'What's got into you?' he asked managing to tear his mouth away from hers.

'Nothing. That's the problem.'

She pushed him back against the wall at arm's length, then caught the hem of the dress and pulled it up over her head. Her tights and the white panties were in her car. She was wearing her bra again, but as she threw the dress aside she reached for the clasp and this time managed to free it with ease. Her breasts quivered as the bra was pulled away.

She saw Tom's eyes staring at her naked body. However puzzled he was at this sudden onslaught, it did not affect his lust. A spark of desire was turning rapidly to flame.

She fell to her knees, caught hold of the sash of material that was knotted around the kimono and undid it; his cock was already tenting the material. Pushing the robe aside, she sank her mouth down on his penis, taking it all, wanting to feel it deep in her throat.

'Christ,' he said, as she sucked him so hard her cheeks were dimpled by the effort. She ran her hand up between his legs and cupped his balls, squeezing them so hard she felt his cock jerk upward.

She had never felt like this. She had lost count of how many orgasms she'd had on Pamela's bed, under the gentle persuasion of her fingers and tongue and the little vibrator, but it was as though all that pleasure had only been a precursor to the main event. This main event.

'God, your mouth's so hot,' he moaned.

It was true. The direct connection between her mouth and her sex was evident again. Both shared the same reason for their heat.

She pulled back until the ridge of his glans was poised at her lips then thrust forward again, so deep she had to control the reflex to gag, his flesh buried in the ribbing of her throat.

'Take it easy,' he said, gripping her shoulders and trying to pull her to her feet.

She allowed his cock to slip from her lips and got to her feet. Immediately he swept her into his arms, cradling her like a baby. He pushed against a door at the end of the hall and carried her into the bedroom. There was a small, wooden-framed double bed. He dropped her on it but she clung to him so that he was pulled down on top of her.

Scissoring her legs apart, she hooked them over his back, digging her high heels into him and levering her sex up until she felt her labia closing over his cock. Immediately, and with all her strength, she slid her body down onto him, and felt that hard, bone-like shaft lance into her body.

And she came. Then and there, her orgasm

exploding before he'd even penetrated her completely. Her body shuddered, wrapping itself around his bone-hard phallus, every nerve and fibre of her being concentrated on the feeling as he drove the rest of the way into her. He filled her completely. She clung to him, squeezing every last drop of feeling out of herself, using the muscles of her vagina as if to crush him completely.

Then, as her orgasm ebbed away, she unhooked her legs and rolled him over onto his back. His cock sprang free momentarily but she grabbed it in her hand, quickly knelt above him and forced it back inside her, dropping her body down on it until she could feel his pelvis grinding against her pubic bone.

'Oh, God, Tom . . .'

She ground her hips from side to side, feeling her swollen clitoris trapped against his body. She pulled almost all the way off him then dropped herself down on his cock with all her weight. She repeated this three or four times, each time producing a huge surge of feeling; each surge took her closer to another climax. She dropped herself on him one last time, squirming herself down with every last ounce of energy, then fell forward as her orgasm broke over her, its power and purpose rooted in the depths of her sex.

Tom was too surprised by this assault to resist. His cock was buried in a throbbing furnace of delight, her heat and wetness sucking him in. As she stopped moving he began, powering into her with all his strength, thrusting his buttocks off the bed, the need she had created now compelling.

Kate felt his cock spasm strongly inside her. 'Are you going to come?' she asked, straightening up.

'Yes,' he hissed.

She wanted to feel his ejaculation. Immediately, she clenched her sex around him. Unfortunately this produced as strong a feeling in her as it did in him and she moaned loudly and fell forward, unable to stay upright.

Wrapping his arms around her, Tom rolled her over onto her back. Then he powered into her faster and even more urgently than he'd done before.

Kate raised her legs in the air, bending her knees and pulling them back towards her chest, wanting to take him as deeply as she could, opening her sex for him, relaxing every muscle to allow him in. She caught his head in her hands and kissed him on the mouth, thrusting her tongue between his lips. His cock jerked strongly against the tight tube of her sex and she felt a jet of semen flow out of him. It was followed by another and another. By the time she felt the third she was coming again too, her orgasm exploding over the crown of his cock, her sex clutching the whole length of his shaft like a fist, wanting to make sure every last drop of semen was squeezed out of him.

'My God, what on earth got into you?' It was the same question he'd asked her in the hall, in the middle of her assault.

Kate grinned rather sheepishly. 'You did,' she lied.

Sharon knocked twice on her office door then came in without waiting to be asked.

'Donald wants to see you, ASAP.'

Donald Dyer was the senior partner and chairman of Dyer and Freeman and ruled with an iron hand in an iron glove. Requests for interviews were acted on immediately.

'Now?' It was nearly the end of the working day. 'What's it all about?'

Sharon shook her head. She was wearing a short blue mini-dress and strappy high heels, and her short but slender legs were sheathed in white tights. The round neck of the dress revealed her small chirpy breasts, held high by a white bra. Her skin had the radiance and sheen of youth. She had a generous mouth and pouting lips. Kate found herself staring at her through new eyes, wondering what it would be like to . . .

'Kate?' Sharon looked worried at the long silence.

'Oh, sorry, miles away.' Kate got to her feet. 'Better go and face the music.'

'Don't think it's bad news, do you?' Sharon looked worried.

Kate shrugged. She walked with Sharon back into the general office then took the lift up to Dyer's office on the floor above. His secretary sat in a small office outside a large rosewood door. 'Go straight in,' she said, smiling.

Kate knocked.

'Come.'

She opened the door.

'Kate, Kate ... come in, my dear. Sit down.' Donald Dyer had a corner office almost four times the size of her own, with a large oak conference table at one end of the room surrounded by six chairs. His desk was modern, a slab of elm varnished and highly polished and supported by legs made from six inch squares of glass bonded together, one on top of the other. Apart from a computer screen and keyboard and a single white telephone, the surface of the desk was completely bare.

Kate sat in the leather wing chair in front of his desk; in contrast to the desk, the chair looked as if it belonged to another age.

'Look, come straight to the point ... Wanted to congratulate you on the Harding settlement. Excellent piece of work. Excellent.' He leant forward, putting his elbows on his desk. 'And I had lunch with George Christie last week. He was not at all pleased, which is also credit to you.'

'Thank you,' Kate said, wondering what was coming next.

'As you know, David Freeman has been think-ing about retiring. With the sort of billings you've been bringing in, I think it's a logical step to think of you as his replacement. We've talked it over. We want to offer you a senior partnership which will, of course, involve a higher participation in the proceeds of all our endeavours. There are other benefits too, naturally: a change of car, a longer period of holidays. We'll give you details of the whole package in due course. And in two years' time, we will be adding your name to the letterheading. Dyer, Freeman and Hailstone. Sounds impressive, I think.'

Kate tried not to let her mouth fall open. She had been confident that she would be made a senior partner in due course, but she had never expected it so quickly. 'That's very . . .' She was at a loss for words. 'I mean . . . well, I'm delighted.'

'Good, good. As I say, we'll let you have it all in writing. Perhaps we should take some time next week and go out to lunch together, the three of us.'

'That would be nice.'

'I'll get my secretary to speak to Sharon. Congratulations, my dear. I think, with your help, Dyer, Freeman and Hailstone will have a great future in the new millennium.'

Kate managed to walk back to her office without mishap though she had no memory of doing so. Her mind was so full of thoughts of the consequences of what Donald had said she wasn't even sure whether she'd taken the lift or the stairs.

'Well?' Sharon asked expectantly, following her in.

'It seems you are going to be the secretary to one of the senior partners,' Kate said.

'Really? That's great. Is it more money?'

'For both of us, yes.'

'Great. Well done. Does it mean I have to change my image?' She looked down at her short skirt.

'No,' Kate said, and she smiled as she looked, too. 'Don't do that.'

'Hello. It's Kate.'

'Kate. How are you?'

'I'm fine. Actually, I'm better than fine. I've just had some very good news.'

It was strange, she supposed. Kate had several alternatives when it came to celebrations. She could have called Tom. She could have called Pamela. The American had made it perfectly clear that she would be only too happy to indulge in a repeat performance. She could have even phoned Sarah and gone out on the town with her, but as she'd driven home she knew exactly how she wanted to celebrate her promotion.

'What sort of good news?'

'Promotion. I'm being made a senior partner.'

'That sounds very impressive.'

'Listen, I know it's short notice, but I've bought a couple of bottles of very good vintage champagne and I wondered if I might bring them over. If you're not busy, that is?'

'Sounds like fun. Come on over.'

'Great.'

Kate put the phone down and walked upstairs, taking the steps two at a time. Her exhilaration at her promotion was matched by her satisfaction at her personal life. She had taken risks. Big risks. She had gone out on a limb emotionally, but it had all been worthwhile. She had freed herself from the conventions that had been wrapped around her like a cage. At least she felt she had, which amounted to the same thing.

Sex had become part of her life. It was all a question of emphasis. Before, although she had enjoyed sex, it had been in the background, a very minor part of her life. Now it was in the forefront of her thoughts. The ease and facility she had for the most tremendous sexual gratification amazed her. It was not only a cause of satisfaction at the most profound physical level; the fact that it was something she had done of her own volition gave her enormous intellectual satisfaction as well. Though the initial impetus had been an accident, she had seized what she saw as an opportunity in both hands and run with it, shaping and controlling it, and chasing down every last possibility.

The results had been spectacular. She would never have believed herself capable of being so totally confident and adept at purely sexual relationships. Before, she had assumed that sex had to be part of something else, of an emotional nexus that included words like love and partnership. Now she realised that with care and intelligence sex would be a thing apart.

What was more, it seemed that the discoveries she had made about herself, and her lack of inhibitions, somehow fed back into her professional life. She felt more confident and able. She deserved her promotion.

How she felt about what had happened with Pamela was slightly more ambiguous. She hadn't sorted out her feelings in that respect. Not that she had any qualms about what she had done, nor would have any about doing it again, in the short term. But somewhere in the back of her mind, she had a nagging doubt. She did not want to turn into a lesbian. In a sense, the extraordinary need the experience had created in her to have a man had helped to prove to her that there was no danger of that. But the blandishments of Pamela's touch, and the incredible feelings the woman had produced in her body, were things that she knew could easily get out of hand.

For the time being, however, she was content to go with the flow, to let her body dictate to her what she did. She hoped she was realistic enough and sensible enough to call a halt when her mind threw up more rational objections for not continuing than her body could offer for carrying on. In fact, she was sure that was precisely what would happen one day. The helter-skelter ride would, inevitably, come to an end. But though she could see the end of the line in theory, in practice, at the crest of one of the highest parts of the ride, she still felt it was a long way off.

Kate stripped off her clothes and stepped into the shower. She stood under the powerful jets of water, adjusting the mixer tap so it was barely warm.

The phone rang as she towelled herself dry.

'Hello?' she said, sitting on the edge of the bed.

'Kate?'

'Yes.' She didn't recognise the voice.

'It's Gerard.'

'Gerard, how are you?' She couldn't remember

giving Gerard her number.

'Hope you don't mind me calling you like this.'

'How did you get my number?'

'An incredible coincidence actually. Donald Dyer is an old friend of mine. I had lunch with him today. I gather congratulations are in order.'

'I still don't . . .'

'He was telling me about his brilliant new senior partner. He mentioned your name and when I asked him to describe you . . . Well, unmistakable. And there aren't many Hailstones in the phone book. You don't mind, do you?'

'No.' She wasn't sure that was true.

'Look, there's only one reason I called. I've got a friend who's having a house party this weekend. Just a few select friends. Very lavish. Big pool. Nothing but the best food and booze. I wondered if you'd like to come. Saturday night. I thought you might well be in the mood to celebrate.'

'Ah . . .'

'Don't worry, I haven't invited Donald. It'll be fun, I promise you.'

'When you say fun, Gerard . . .'

'I leave that to your imagination, my dear, which I know is graphic.'

It certainly was. Kate saw throngs of nubile girls cavorting by the pool in postage stamp-sized bikinis.

'Can I think about it?'

'Of course. And if you'd like to bring a friend, the more the merrier. Give me a ring tomorrow.'

'I will.'

They said their goodbyes.

Kate walked into her dressing room. The sound of Gerard's voice had revived all sorts of memories. A now familiar pulse of feeling made her shudder.

Knowing Gerard's interests, it was likely that the party was going to be far from conventional, but she didn't want to think about that now. She had other things on her mind.

She opened a drawer in one of the built in wardrobes and extracted a black bustier. It was one of the items she had bought on her shopping expedition in Bond Street. It was made from tulle and was boned so it clinched in tightly at the waist.

Wrapping it around her body, Kate secured the hooks into the tightest of the three sets of eyes that ran down the back. A criss-cross pattern of red laces decorated the front and long, delicately ruched red satin suspenders hung down to her thighs. The garment tucked under her breasts but did not cover them; its hem, delicately frilled with lace, sat on top of her hips.

Kate took out a pair of black stockings, unhooked a bright red silk dress from the rail and picked out a pair of black high heels. She walked back into the bedroom, sat on the bed and rolled the stockings up her legs, clipping them into the suspenders of the bustier, each little metal ring and rubber nub covered with a diagonal sash of red satin.

She stood up and climbed into the heels. Standing with her arms akimbo in front of the mirror she stared at the way the lingerie had transformed her body. The hem of the bustier, the long red suspenders and the jet-black welts of the stockings neatly framed her belly and the vertical stripe of her pubic hair, drawing attention to it – attention it craved. She felt her clitoris throb sharply and resisted the temptation to run her hand down between her legs. She turned and looked over her shoulder. The high heels shaped and firmed her legs, her pert buttocks pouting out from the top of her thighs, her calves hard and shapely, the Achilles tendon on her ankles pinched and thin. She looked like an expensive whore waiting for a generous client.

The thought made her grin.

She slipped into the dress. It had a high collar but was sleeveless, the material fitted to the waist then flaring slightly at the hips. The skirt of the dress was only just long enough to hide the tops of the black stockings.

Kate went back into her dressing room and began to put on her make-up.

'Hi.'

'Hi.' Kate held up the two bottles of Krug she'd bought at the local wine shop on the way home from work.

'Come in. What a sexy outfit.'

'Thanks. Sexy was the general idea.'

Marianne took the champagne from her and led her into the sitting room. Three tall champagne flutes sat on a tray on the coffee table together with a large silver ice bucket filled with ice. Marianne dropped a bottle into it.

'I thought I'd better be prepared.' She began twisting the cork off the other bottle. 'This is wonderful.'

'You look pretty sexy too.' Marianne was wearing a short cream dress that seemed to float around her body as if it had a life of its own. She wasn't wearing tights or shoes and her long blonde hair was brushed out and loose, tumbling over her shoulders in waves.

'Thank you.' The cork came out with a pop. Marianne poured the fizzing liquid into two glasses and handed Kate one. They clinked them together then sipped the wine.

'Here's to your promotion, then,' she said.

'Where's Peter?'

'Oh, he's just called to say he's going to be a bit late. Business.'

'I don't even know what he does,' Kate said, thinking aloud.

'He's in advertising. He's showing some client the storyboards for a new campaign. It all had to be changed suddenly. He shouldn't be long. So what's this new job of yours going to mean?'

'Power, status, money. Little things like that. I'm going to get my name on the shingle too.'

'Shingle?'

'Dyer, Freeman and Hailstone.'

'Which one are you?'

Kate realised she hadn't used her surname before. 'Hailstone.'

'But that's not the only reason you've come.' It

was not a question. Marianne had sat in the corner of the sofa and drawn her legs up underneath her. Instead of choosing the opposite sofa, Kate sat beside her.

'No. It's not.'

'What then?'

'How strict is your rule?' The front of Marianne's dress was loose and Kate could see she wasn't wearing a bra. If she cared to look she could see one of the blonde's small pink nipples.

'About what?' Marianne leant forward to pick up the champagne flute. Kate could see both her breasts as the dress fell forward.

'You being with a woman.'

'Very. Otherwise it's like having an affair.'

'What about if it's a woman Peter has already been to bed with?'

'That's never happened.'

'And if it did?'

Marianne looked puzzled and confused. 'I don't see what you're getting at.'

Kate put down her glass. She twisted round to face Marianne, put one hand on her knee and the other on her cheek and kissed her lightly on the lips. The astonishment on Marianne's face was obvious. Kate kissed her again, this time darting her tongue out to lick her lower lip and running her hand up under her skirt to caress her thigh.

'What's got into you?'

She'd heard that question before. 'Let's just say I'm in the mood to experiment.'

Marianne uncurled her legs and sat up.

'Experiment with me?'

'Yes.' Kate leant forward. 'Do you find the idea unappealing?'

'I find it very appealing.'

'Well, then.' Kate's hand patted Marianne's thigh lightly. 'But I don't want to break any rules.'

'This has never happened before.'

'How long will Peter be?'

'I don't know. Let me call him on his mobile.'

'What a good idea.'

Kate watched Marianne cross the room. There was a phone on a drinks cabinet beside the large dining room table. Marianne picked it up and punched in a number.

Kate got to her feet and walked up to the blonde. She smiled at her then stooped and kissed her on the mouth again, pushing her back against the table. This time the kiss was much harder and she felt Marianne respond. As Kate's tongue ventured between her lips, Marianne's danced against it. She gave a little gasp of pleasure as Kate's body crushed against hers.

Kate lowered her mouth to Marianne's neck. She could hear Peter's phone ringing in the earpiece. She sucked on the corded flesh of Marianne's neck, as her hand covered her left breast. It was small but, judging from the way Marianne's body shuddered, very sensitive. She tweaked the nipple hard as her mouth descended over her collar-bone. She pushed the material of the dress to one side and managed to suck on her right nipple. She could encompass the whole of her breast with her

201

mouth.

Her hands dropped to the skirt of the dress and pulled it up to Marianne's hips. The blonde was wearing white cotton panties.

'What are you doing?' Marianne hissed, though it was perfectly obvious.

Kate did not reply. She hooked her hands under Marianne's thighs and lifted her until she was sitting on the edge of the table then spread her legs apart. She dropped to her knees between them and kissed the gusset of the panties where it stretched across the plane of Marianne's sex.

'Hello?' Peter sounded distant.

Marianne moaned loudly as Kate squirmed her mouth against her labia. She lay back on the table top, the phone still held to her ear.

'Hello? Who is this?'

'Peter.'

'Who is this?'

Marianne's voice sounded strained. Kate wasn't surprised he didn't recognise it. She raised her hand and pulled the cotton crotch aside. To her astonishment, Marianne's sex was hairless, the whole area shaved clean, though there was a tiny downy blonde triangle on her mons, its lower angle just touching the crease of her sex. Her labia were thin and incredibly smooth and moist, as though they had been oiled with some exotic perfumed unguent. Kate pressed her mouth forward onto it, and ran her tongue up and down between her labia.

'Oh, no . . .' Marianne said. She stretched her

spare hand out to try and push Kate away but it was only a token resistance.

Kate could hear Peter's voice in the earpiece again. 'Who is this? What's going on?'

'Peter, it's me,' Marianne managed to say.

Kate flattened her mouth against Marianne's sex, splaying her labia apart. She worked her tongue up to the blonde's clitoris, feeling it throbbing as she did so.

'Darling, how are you? Are you all right? You sound ill.'

'Kate's here.'

Kate tapped at Marianne's clitoris, turning the tip of her tongue into a little hammer. Marianne's body shuddered. Kate moved her hand under Marianne's buttocks and slipped her fingers into the lower part of her labia. Considering she was new to all this, she was pleased at her own adeptness.

'So what's the problem?'

'We wondered . . . Oh, Christ . . .'

The latter response had been produced by Kate's fingers. She had thrust two of them into Marianne's vagina. It was already hot and very sticky. Kate felt her own body register a wave of excitement.

'What's the matter, darling?' The reception on the phone had improved and Peter's voice sounded concerned.

'How long will you be, Peter?' Marianne asked, trying to concentrate on what she was saying.

'Tell me what's wrong, darling.'

'It's Kate. Our rules. You know our . . . Oh . . .'

Kate managed to thrust her fingers forward an extra inch, crushing her knuckles into Marianne's slick labia. At the same time her tongue pressed Marianne's clitoris back against the bone, then dragged it from side to side.

'Kate what?' Peter sounded annoyed now.

'Kate wants to go to bed . . .'

'I realise that . . .'

'With me. Oh Peter, for Christ's sake, get home. It's just so good.'

'What are you doing?'

'She's got me on the dining room table. She's licking my clit. God, I feel like I'm on fire.'

'I won't be long.'

'Oh no . . .'

Kate replaced her tongue with her finger. As she skittered it across Marianne's clitoris at the same tempo, she pulled her other fingers out of her vagina and pushed her tongue into it, straining it as far forward as it would go. Marianne tasted sweet.

'Tell me,' Peter said insistently. 'Tell me what she's doing to you.'

'She's got her finger on my clit and her tongue's right up inside me. God, Peter, she's going to make me come.'

'It's all right,' he said reassuringly. 'Let it happen.'

Kate twisted her tongue around, stretching the elastic flesh at the mouth of Marianne's vagina. She could feel Marianne's clitoris throbbing violently under her finger and knew she was going to come.

The phone had gone dead. Marianne dropped it onto the table. Kate felt her thighs pressing in on her cheeks, the pressure in Marianne's body building.

'You're making me come,' Marianne moaned. Suddenly, her whole body jerked, like it had been struck by lightning. She arched up from the table, every muscle rigid, then, as if in slow motion, sank back down again. Her clitoris spasmed wildly and Kate felt a gush of juices running from her sex, almost as if she'd ejaculated like a man. Her thighs went limp, releasing their grip on Kate's face.

'What did Peter say?' Kate asked, getting to her feet. Her mouth was wet with Marianne's juices.

'He said to start without him.'

'I think we already have.'

It was Marianne's turn to take the initiative. She rolled off the table and pulled the cream dress over her head. She skimmed the panties down and kicked them aside.

'Do you shave it?' Kate asked, looking at the tiny triangle of pubic hair. Marianne's sex was angled outward and Kate could also see the first two inches of her labia, the skin smooth and buttery.

'Yes. Every day. Otherwise it would get all rough. I like to oil it, too. God, you've made me so randy. This is not what I expected.' She took one step forward, put one arm around Kate's waist and kissed her on the lips, licking at her own juices enthusiastically. 'I can taste myself. That's so sexy. Hey, what are you wearing?' she said as her fingers explored Kate's waist.

'I was feeling sluttish,' Kate said. 'Unzip me.'

Marianne moved behind her and pulled down the zip, then pushed the dress off Kate's shoulders. As Kate pulled her arms clear it fell to the floor. Marianne stared at the black bustier and the long ruched suspenders. 'My God ... Peter'll come on the spot if he sees you in that.'

'You like it, then?' One of the stockings had wrinkled slightly at the knee. Kate put her foot up on the seat of a dining chair and used the palms of both hands to smooth the nylon back into place, adjusting the suspenders to hold it more tightly.

'Are you going to tell me what brought all this on?' Marianne asked. As she said it, she moved her hand to cup one of Kate's breasts. She caressed it delicately, running her palm over the nipple. 'God, I'd love to have tits like this.'

The blonde dipped her head. Taking the soft flesh between her fingers, she guided the nipple into her mouth. It was her turn to push Kate back against the edge of the table. Kate felt a huge surge of feeling as Marianne's teeth grazed her nipple. Then her lips sucked at the flesh, pulling it outward and coating it with saliva. She transferred her mouth to the other breast and repeated the same procedure, except, this time, after sucking the nipple out, she pushed it back in with the tip of her tongue, burying it in the surrounding flesh until it was pressed back against Kate's ribs.

206

'What about Peter?' Kate said hoarsely.

Marianne raised her head and kissed Kate on the lips, pushing her back onto the top of the table. As Kate felt the cold wooden surface against her back, Marianne climbed onto the table too, lying beside her.

The blonde's lips nuzzled Kate's neck and throat, then worked up to her ear. She blew hot air into the inner whorls. 'God, I'm so turned on. This has never happened before. I can't believe it's happening now. I wanted you so much, watching you with Peter. After you'd gone, he was like a wild man, but I couldn't get you out of my mind.'

Her hand ran down over the black tulle. Kate felt it on her belly. The fingers curved around her pubic bone, the whole hand pressed flat against the hot wet labia. 'Like this, is this what you want?' Marianne said. While her other fingers remained stationary, pressing the labia back against the bone, her middle finger slipped downward into the slick wetness between them. It found her clitoris and wriggled up against it.

Kate moaned loudly. Since she got into her car to drive home, that was what she'd been imagining. The wonderful thing about her life at the moment was not only did she know exactly what she wanted, she also had the means of getting it – and almost instantly.

Marianne slipped off the table without taking her hand away. As her finger squirmed against Kate's clitoris, pushing it this way and that, she spread Kate's legs apart and knelt between them, pulling her to the edge of the table until her buttocks were half over it and her sex was suspended in mid-air. Ducking down she forced her shoulders up under Kate's thighs and stared at her vulva. The skimpy black pubic hair between Kate's legs hid nothing.

'Is this what you want?' she repeated.

'Yes. Oh, God, yes.'

Even if she hadn't replied, Kate was sure Marianne could see for herself how desperately excited she was. Her pussy was wet. She could feel her juices running down between her buttocks.

'Like this . . .'

Marianne's fingers splayed apart, drawing Kate's labia apart too. Kate felt a breath of hot air playing over the inner surfaces as the blonde blew on it gently. Then she sank her mouth down on it hungrily, her tongue worming its way against Kate's clitoris.

Kate's body shuddered, a huge wave of pleasure coursing through it. Somewhere very distantly she heard the noise of a door being opened and closed very gently but was too involved to pay more than a second's fleeting attention to it. The initial impact of Marianne's mouth had forced her eyes closed and it was physically impossible to open them again. She knew that she was coming; that was all that mattered.

'Don't stop,' she pleaded weakly.

Marianne didn't. Her tongue began a relentless rhythm, moving up and down, touching every single nerve in her clitoris and making every one react. A hundred different tingling pleasures began to combine into one.

Another noise. Louder. Nearer.

Kate turned her head toward it but lost interest as a renewed wave of sensation washed over her.

'Oh, God.' She was coming. She stretched her arms across the table and caught hold of the table edge, her fingers clutching at it for support as her body began to spasm. She felt her vagina clench but as she teetered on the brink, her orgasm no more than hairbreadth away, she felt Marianne's tongue falter momentarily and the angle of her mouth change, though it was still clamped firmly to Kate's sex.

Kate struggled to open her eyes. Peter was standing behind his wife, a big erection jutting out from his shirt-tails, his trousers around his knees. He had pulled Marianne to her feet so she was bent over with her buttocks pointing back at him.

'So this is what you get up to when I'm away,' he said with his teeth gritted. He took hold of her naked hips and pushed his cock up between her legs. Instantly Kate felt an explosion of hot air against her sex, as Marianne's silent exclamation bore testimony to her husband's searching penetration. Then, as Kate felt Peter's body battering into his wife, Marianne's tongue began to move again.

It was an extraordinary sensation. She seemed to be able to feel Peter's cock through the medium of Marianne's body. Every stroke made Marianne's tongue tremble and her mouth melt. The heat was incredible. The sudden shock of Peter's presence, the erotic spectacle he presented and this new sensation all combined to send Kate hurtling into orgasm. Her body arched up off the table, every nerve and sinew strained with pleasure. She was screaming, too – a noise she did not recognise, strangulated and unearthly.

'Did you dress her like this?' she heard Peter say before she had the energy to move.

'No. It was all her own idea.'

Kate felt Marianne's mouth move away. She opened her eyes and saw the blonde come to stand at her side. Her lips were wet, she licked them with her tongue, then leant forward and kissed Kate delicately.

'That was so good,' she said quietly.

'I know.'

'And what about this?' Peter added loudly. He hooked his hands under Kate's thighs, pulled them up to waist level, stepped between them and in one seamless movement drove his penis right up into Kate's soaking wet vagina.

Despite all the experiences she had had in recent weeks, Kate didn't think she had ever felt anything like that. His penis was red-hot, like a poker left in the fire for too long, but it was big, too. Bigger and harder than it had been last time, his passion aroused by what he had seen. It was stroking into her with all his strength too, powering up and down with incredible force, his glans hammering at the neck of her womb, his pubic bone crushing her already tenderised clitoris. She thought she could feel him pulsing too, his semen pumping into his cock ready for his ejaculation.

This was exactly why she had wanted to be with them tonight. After her experience with Pamela and the subsequent desperate need she had felt for a man, being with Peter and Marianne was the perfect solution. After the wonderful softness of Marianne's mouth, the subtlety and finesse of a woman, the desire for the hardness and power of a man could be fulfilled instantly. She wanted both. And these days, she was used to getting exactly what she wanted.

Her body was on fire, blazing with a thousand different sensations, her sex stretched in every direction by the size of the organ that filled it so completely. But her mind was running wild too, filled with images of what they would do to her later. This was only the beginning, after all, the foreplay. She was dressed for sex. She wanted to parade in front of them, provoke them, kiss them both, suck them both, let them watch as she masturbated, let them do whatever they wanted with her, let them enjoy sharing one woman between the two of them.

She looked up at Marianne. The blonde bent down to kiss her lips. She slid one hand over Kate's breast, and the other down over her belly, between the labia that her husband's cock had spread so wide apart, and onto her clitoris. With the lightest of touches she rolled her finger over it.

Kate moaned. She felt her sex clutching at the huge phallus that slammed into her and her clitoris dancing under Marianne's touch. She felt her nipple being lifted and pinched, dragging the rest of her breast upward too. And then Peter pulled her towards him with all his strength, slamming into her one final time, not retreating again but jerking wildly as his semen flowed out of him, jet after jet of it. For a second Kate's body was in stasis, as though there was just too much to cope with. Then she felt it screw itself around the hard bone-like phallus and she came again in great gushing pulses, as if her orgasm was answering his blow for blow, every spasm of his cock returned in equal measure by spasms in her own.

Chapter Ten

'*SO WHAT'S HE* like?'

'A bit weird.'

'Weird? What haven't you told me?'

'Have another glass of wine.'

'No. I don't want to get drunk before we get there.'

'He should be here any minute.' Kate got to her feet and walked over to the front window. It was ten to eight.

'Don't change the subject, what's he like?'

'Oh, he's charming and quite fanciable.'

'So why weird?'

'He likes to play games.'

'What sort of games? Sex games?'

Kate wished she'd hadn't been so frank. 'Yes.'

'And you think this party might be . . .'

'It's possible.'

'Oh, sounds terrific. I love all that.'

'Do you?'

'Mmm.' Instead of wanting to hide her plumpness, Sarah was wearing an impossibly tight dress that clung to every curve. It was strapless, revealing a blossoming cleavage, and had a short skirt that displayed her thighs. The bright pink material was some sort of stretchy Lycra into which thousands of tiny pink sequins had been sewn. She wore flesh-coloured tights and ankle-strap pink patent leather high heels, which added inches to her height, and a heavy make-up with almost scarlet eye-shadow. 'So listen are you two together?'

'Together?'

'An item?'

'No, not at all. Feel free.'

'In that case I will. He sounds right up my street.'

Kate had decided that if she were going to accept Gerard's invitation to the party, she didn't want to go alone. When she'd described the event to Sarah on the phone on Friday morning, telling her word for word what Gerard had said, her friend had been intrigued and excited and had agreed to accompany her without any hesitation. Gerard had been delighted at the news and had told her he'd pick them up at eight.

Kate had chosen her most extravagant evening dress, a concoction of gold lamé, sleeveless with a mandarin collar under which the dress was split all the way down to the waist, making it impossible for her to wear a bra. Its ankle-length skirt was tight with a kick-pleat at the back, the gold material clinging to the curves of her bottom, hips and thighs. She wore gold high-heeled sandals and black tights interwoven with a gold thread. She had even found a little gold glitter to brush into her eye-shadow. With her hair trimmed into a perfect shape in her lunch break yesterday, she looked, she knew, at her very best.

She felt at her best, too. She might have expected to be exhausted by what had happened with Marianne and Peter. Instead, the experience seemed to have invigorated her. It was, she supposed, the ultimate. It was obvious that sex with a woman – sex with Pamela and Marianne – was always going to be completely different from sex with a man, but she had never imagined how different. The tenderness of a woman's touch, the melting softness of their bodies pressed against her own, and the way it seemed possible not only to feel the sensations they created in her but to experience just as acutely the sensations she created in them, had given sex a whole new dimension. But it had also left her feeling something else. Even with Pamela, who had used the dildo, her vagina had been neglected, unused and uncared for. That was what had produced her longing for a man. To be able to have both, to follow the knowing caresses of a woman with the power and hardness of a man, was simply unbelievable. As Peter had plunged his rock-hard erection into her body after it had been so beautifully pampered by his wife, Kate had come to know the meaning of the word ecstasy. Finishing one of the bottles of Krug, they had taken the second bottle up to the bedroom and found that the experience could be repeated with equal passion.

215

'What are you thinking about?' Sarah asked.

Kate was standing staring out of the window. 'Nothing.'

'So did you go through with it?'

'Go through with what?'

'Remember? Our conversation. You were thinking of bonking a woman, weren't you?'

Kate turned and looked at her friend. Sarah's plump face was creased in a grin. 'He's here.' Just as she was deciding what to say, the highly polished Rolls-Royce glided to a halt in front of her house and double-parked in the street. The blond chauffeur raced around to open the passenger door and Gerard climbed out. He was wearing evening dress and a black bow tie. He bounded up the front steps and rang the bell.

Sarah got to her feet. 'Saved by the bell. But I want to hear about it all, later.'

Kate smiled. 'Good. Because I'd like to talk about it, too.' Kate walked into the hall and opened the front door.

'My God, look at you,' Gerard said, his eyes widening. 'You look magnificent. Piers is going to be impressed.'

'Well, thank you. Come in for a moment.' She led him into the sitting room. 'This is my friend Sarah. Sarah, Gerard.'

'Absolutely charmed, my dear.' He looked it; his eyes roamed Sarah's plump curves with obvious appreciation.

Sarah got to her feet. As he kissed her on both cheeks, Sarah winked over his shoulder and mouthed the word, 'Gorgeous,' at Kate.

'What a lovely car,' Sarah said.

'You both look quite devastating. If you don't mind, we'd better make tracks.'

'Of course.' Kate gathered up her tiny gold evening bag, set the burglar alarm and opened the front door. Outside, as Gerard shepherded Sarah into the car, Kate locked the door and dropped the keys into her bag.

The blond chauffeur stood holding the passenger door open. As Kate approached, he remained perfectly passive, his expression giving nothing away. Kate got to the threshold of the car, with the thick door between them, and looked him straight in the eye. If it had been him in that strange room in Gerard's house, if he had been the one who had used her so intimately, he gave not the slightest sign of it.

'A thorn between two roses,' Gerard said, as Kate climbed into the car and sat on Gerard's left while Sarah was already squeezed in at his right.

'So who is this Piers?' Kate asked as the chauffeur got behind the wheel and the car glided silently down the road.

'Piers Lindsay, the Viscount of Addingham, you must have heard of him.'

'That Piers,' Kate said. Hardly a day went by without Viscount Addingham appearing in the gossip columns of the newspapers, usually accompanied by a nubile and scantily clad beauty. A year ago, his extremely beautiful young wife had divorced him in a court case that had made the front pages of all the tabloids: she claimed she had returned from a shopping expedition and found him in bed with two women, one of whom was a countess and the other a prostitute. She had given evidence that he had repeatedly made what she regarded as excessive sexual demands and had frequently asked her to share a bed with other women.

'You mustn't believe everything you read in the newspapers,' Gerard said.

'What sort of party is this going to be, Gerard?' Sarah asked.

'You'll see,' Gerard replied, tapping the side of his nose with his finger.

'Sounds like it's going to be fun.' Sarah squeezed Gerard's knee.

'Oh, I can guarantee you fun.'

Kate wasn't sure whether the news of where they were going made her feel foreboding or excitement. Undoubtedly, a few weeks ago she would have demanded to be taken straight home. Now she felt differently. She was no longer afraid of her own sexuality. What was more, she was curious to meet Piers Lindsay. From his photographs he was an attractive man – an attraction that was clearly felt by his many female admirers. He also had a reputation for providing lavish entertainment and it would certainly be interesting to see how the other half lived.

The car headed out to the west, its soft suspension and whisper-quiet engine making the journey almost soporific. Gerard appeared to be totally smitten with Sarah, asking her an endless stream of questions about her life and spending a great deal of time looking down the front of her dress, her cleavage and thighs exerting a seemingly hypnotic attraction.

After a few miles of motorway the car turned off to the left and was soon wending its way down a narrow country lane. Ten or fifteen minutes later, it arrived at a pair of tall wrought-iron gates supported by brick pillars and set in an ancient red-brick wall. A young man in a red jacket stood in front of the gates. He was holding a clipboard.

Gerard wound down the electric window and leant forward. 'Gerard Manners, party of three,' he said.

The young man consulted the clipboard, made a tick with his pen, and examined the inside of the car carefully, checking there were no stowaways perhaps. Satisfied that all was in order, he said, 'Thank you, sir.' He went to a small computer pad that was screwed into the brick pillar on the left-hand side and keyed in four numbers.

The big gates swung open. As soon as they had driven through they closed again.

'Piers likes his privacy,' Gerard said. 'You know what the press are like, these days.'

The car swept up a gravel driveway. The gardens were beautifully landscaped with some very old cedars and oaks and a lot of large shrubs, the tall brick wall surrounding them completely. They drove up to a superb Queen Anne house, its carriage driveway surmounted by a large fountain.

As the Rolls glided to a halt, Kate saw a selection of other very expensive cars: a Ferrari, two Mercedes, a Porsche and at least three other Rolls-Royces, parked in an area at the side of the house.

The chauffeur climbed out of the car and opened the passenger door.

Kate got out first. Standing in front of the large panelled front door was an attractive blonde. She was wearing an incredibly tight white satin strapless and heavily boned body, its legs cut so high the crease of her pelvis was visible, the wired bra at the top pushing her large breasts upward and out. Her long slender legs were encased in white fishnet tights and she wore white calf-length high-heeled boots.

'Mr Manners, good evening, sir,' she said, smiling broadly.

'Good evening, Gloria. You're looking quite wonderful, as usual.'

'Thank you, sir. Would you like to come this way?'

The blonde opened the front door and led the way into a large vestibule. There was a sweeping staircase up to a first-floor landing on the right, its newel post carved with a coat of arms. To the left, the girl opened a door and indicated that they should go through.

It was not what Kate had expected. She had imagined a party teeming with hundreds of guests. Instead, about twenty people stood in an L-shaped sitting room, mostly drinking champagne served by three girls wearing identical costumes to the girl outside. There were five women, all parading the latest evening dresses from the fashion houses of Versace, St Laurent and Lagerfield, but the rest of the guests were men, all in black evening dress.

'Gerry, old boy, glad you could come.'

Piers Lindsay was, if anything, more attractive than his photographs. He was tall and slender with very black hair, a thick lock of which fell over his forehead periodically and was brushed back with a shake of the head. He had eyes that were so brown they were almost black and high, hollow cheekbones. His nose was straight and he had a fleshy sensuous mouth that seemed to be slightly out of synch with the words he spoke.

'Piers, this is Sarah and Kate.'

Piers kissed Sarah on both cheeks with elaborate formality. Then he turned to Kate and did the same. 'That dress is wonderful on you,' he said, his eyes tracing the shimmering gold from her neck to her ankles, pausing at her bosom where her breasts edged against the dramatic split that ran down to her waist.

'Thank you,' she said.

Piers, like Gerard, was wearing evening dress but with a white jacket and a scarlet bow-tie and matching cummerbund.

'I'm so glad you could come.' He gazed straight into Kate's eyes. She had the impression she was the only woman in the room, his complete attention focused on her. 'Gerry told me you're a solicitor. What do you specialise in?'

'Insurance, mostly.'

'How interesting. Here, let's get you some champagne.'

One of the girls arrived with a tray of glasses and Piers distributed them to his guests. Two other men detached themselves from the crowd and were introduced. They, like Gerard, appeared fascinated by Sarah's cleavage.

'Let me show you the buffet,' Piers said, taking Kate's elbow and walking her into the other part of the room. Three long tables were weighed down with food, each with a different course. There were starters on the first: salads, caviar, oysters, huge prawns, plates of Parma ham and asparagus, smoked salmon and salami. The middle one displayed lobsters, cold salmon and various hot dishes in a silver *bain marie*. The third was set out with tarts, cold bavarois, fresh fruit, and extravagant gateaux, as well as huge circular plates of *petits fours*. Two chefs in tall toques presided over each table, helping guests to load their plates.

'If you can bear to hold back your hunger, I'd love to show you the pool.'

'And I'd love to see it.' Whatever the newspapers had written about him, they had not mentioned his charm and Kate found herself responding to it.

He led her out through a bank of French windows to a stone paved patio, which was dotted with large terracotta pots filled with busy lizzies. Beyond it was a large rectangular swimming pool, one end of which had been made into a waterfall, the water cascading from a thickly planted terrace above. Two girls were swimming lengths in the blue water; neither was wearing a swimsuit.

'It's beautiful.'

'Now come and meet some of the others.'

They walked back inside. Piers took her over to a group of men and introduced her, then insisted on taking her back to the buffet, pointing out what she should have. The caviar was Beluga, he told her, and was a must. She allowed him to spoon quantities onto her plate.

People milled around, smiling and talking. Piers excused himself to greet another guest, a single man, and Kate found herself talking to one of the female guests.

'Charming, isn't he?' she said. 'I'm Patsy, by the way.' The woman was a redhead. She was wearing a full-length backless green dress with a halter neck and a large emerald pinned over her rather small breasts.

'Kate, and yes, he's very charming.'

'You haven't been before, have you?'

'No.'

'Who introduced you?'

'Gerard.' She pointed towards Gerard, who was helping Sarah to select her first course.

'Oh, Gerry. He's always here. He's got a wicked imagination; I think that's why Piers invites him.'

'Sorry about that,' Piers said, arriving back at Kate's side. 'That's the last of the guests.'

'I expected more people,' she said.

'Really? Here, let's get you some lobster.'

223

They ate the main course and talked to the other guests. Kate glimpsed Sarah across the room with Gerard at her elbow and winked at her. The blonde winked back, miming some words Kate could not understand. The champagne was replaced by red or white wine, both of an outstanding vintage.

It was not until most people had finished eating and the plates and food were cleared away that Kate noticed anything out of the ordinary. Piers had introduced her to a tall, gangling man who worked in advertising and the three of them were standing talking on the patio outside the French windows. It was a warm balmy night, and the whole area was floodlit now that the sun had set; the underwater lights of the pool caught the spray from a single male swimmer and turned it into a thousand tiny prisms.

There were several comfortable wicker loungers and chairs on the patio and Kate's eye was caught by one of the male guests, stretched out on one of them. A waitresses had brought him a glass of champagne but he had pulled her down to sit beside him and was pushing his hand into the tight bra of her outfit, cupping his fingers around her breast. She seemed totally unconcerned at this intrusion.

'Would you like some coffee,' Piers asked her, 'or something else to drink?'

He had attended to her every need all evening. 'Yes, thanks.'

When they stepped back inside, the first two tables had been emptied of food and the chefs had gone. A heated tray held silver pots of coffee.

'Black, please,' Kate said, as he picked up the pot.

She glanced around looking for Sarah. She was nowhere to be seen. Gerard too had disappeared, as had about half of the guests. In the corner, Gloria, the girl who had guarded the front door, was sitting on a small cream-coloured sofa. As Kate watched, a man, his bow-tie undone and the top button of his shirt open, came up behind her. He ran his hands over her bare shoulders and down to the top of the breasts, then burrowed into the stiff bra. As he did so, another balding and portly man knelt at her feet. Gloria raised her leg and rested her calf on his shoulder. Kate saw her saying something to him, but was too far away to hear what it was. The man immediately dipped his head and began licking the shiny white satin that was stretched tautly between her legs.

Piers followed Kate's eyes. 'She's a beautiful girl, isn't she?' he asked casually, as if it was perfectly normal for her to be assailed by two men in this way. 'But then, they all are, don't you think?'

'Yes,' Kate said absently, not at all sure how she should respond.

'I see Gerry's gone already. How long have you known him?'

'Not long.'

One of the women guests, a long-haired blonde wearing a full-sleeved high-collared black dress with a long skirt, was talking to a man and another

225

woman in a short pleated white dress with a plunging neckline. Again, they were too far away for Kate to hear what they were talking about, but the man seemed to be pointing to the blonde's chest. Casually the other woman raised her hand and cupped it over the blonde's left breast. The man then moved behind her, unzipped the dress and pulled it down her arms and off her shoulders. It dropped to the floor. The woman stepped out of it. She was wearing a black lace basque and black stockings but no panties. Kate found herself staring at her thick delta of pubic hair. The man ran his hand around her belly and began stroking it, as the other woman stepped forward and kissed the blonde lightly on the lips.

There was no doubt in Kate's mind now that these were not individual incidents of uncontrollable lust but calculated and planned events. The food and wine were merely an aperitif to the main business of the evening.

She had suspected something of the sort after Gerard's telephoned invitation. In the car, her suspicions had been further enhanced. But now, faced with the truth, her reactions were less ambiguous than they had been earlier. It might have been because of Piers and the attraction she felt for him, or because sex was so close to the top of her agenda these days that her sexual appetite could be easily aroused, or even because the blonde in the black basque was now kissing the woman in the short white dress so passionately that it reminded Kate of what Pamela and

Marianne had done to her. Whatever the reason, Kate found her response was an almost breathtaking surge of excitement.

Suddenly, everywhere she looked there were similar incidents. To her right, and only a few yards away, one of the waitresses knelt in front of a rather corpulent male guest, unzipping his trousers and extracting his cock from his fly. She slipped it into her mouth. Patsy, the redhead, stood at his side.

'Shall we take this one upstairs?' Patsy asked him, nodding towards the kneeling girl.

'I thought you wanted her,' the man replied. His head indicated Kate.

Patsy looked into Kate's eyes. 'She's new. I think Piers has *droit de seigneur*.' She raised her voice in case Piers hadn't heard. 'Isn't that right, Piers?'

'Definitely,' he said. He took Kate's arm by the elbow. 'I can be very possesive,' he whispered.

Trying to keep her voice flat and calm, she said, 'The waitresses are—'

'Provided for my guests. I pick each one personally.' He grinned, like a child caught doing something he knew he shouldn't. That explained why there were more men than women. 'I designed the costume myself, too.'

'And am I your partner for tonight?' she asked.

'Gerard explained, didn't he?' Piers looked mildly alarmed.

'Explained what?'

'About all this. Our little . . . group.'

'Oh yes,' she lied.

'Good. Let's go upstairs, then. I have to say, Gerard always seems to turn up with the most beautiful women. I don't know how he does it.'

Kate did. Through the columns of 'Kindred Spirits'.

Piers guided her through to the vestibule. One of the waitresses was kneeling halfway up the stairs. Presumably the extensive view of her buttocks provided by the high-cut legs of the white body had been too much for her male companion. He had grabbed her, pulled the zip at the back of the garment down and wriggled it over her hips so he could get access to her sex, and was now busily pounding his large erection into her. As they passed them on the staircase Kate glanced down. The white fishnet tights had no crotch, an opening between the legs allowing easy access on occasions such as this.

'This way,' Piers said, taking her hand.

On the first-floor landing he led her down a long corridor with doors on either side. Some of the doors were closed and others wide open.

'Take your time,' Piers said. 'A closed door is for those who prefer a little privacy. An open one means open house.'

Kate stopped at the first open door they came to because she recognised the frizzy hair of the blonde who was kneeling on the bed. It was Sarah. The front of her dress had been pulled down and the skirt pulled up and a large, muscular man was ploughing his phallus into her from behind. Gerard, meantime, was kneeling at the other end

228

of her body with his cock firmly embedded in her mouth, her head bobbing up and down on it. Her breasts slapped against her chest as her body was rocked by the man's powerful thrusts.

Piers took Kate's hand and led her away. The next door was closed but Kate thought she heard an odd thwacking sound, followed by a yelp of pain.

The next door was closed, too, but the fourth was open and Kate felt her pulse start to race as she saw what was happening on the bed. One of the waitresses, her white satin outfit discarded, but the conveniently designed fishnet tights still in place, was lying on her back on the bed. Her face was buried in the sex of the woman who crouched above her, grinding herself down on the girl's mouth.

'Piers, darling,' she said. 'Just what I need.'

'I can see you're having a good time, Melissa,' he said.

'Oh, come on, Piers, come and join us.' Piers shook his head, but not altogether to Kate's relief. The sight of the two women had made Kate's sex throb wildly.

Melissa lent forward, spread the waitress's legs apart with her hands and began to lick her labia extravagantly from top to bottom. After a moment of this, she focused her mouth on the upper labia, her tongue burrowing down on the girl's clitoris. Kate had to suppress a moan as her body remembered vividly the feeling of being assailed in this way.

Piers led her away again. 'My room,' he said, opening a door at the far end of the hall. He pulled Kate inside, turned, gathered her up in his arms and kissed her full on the mouth. Kate responded at once. If she felt any resentment at Gerard for not telling her exactly what she was letting herself in for, and laying her on for Piers as the 'new girl', this was not the time to express it. Her ravening sexual appetites came first. Kissing Piers back, she wormed her body against him. His hand felt for the zip of the dress. She heard it sing as he ran it down her back. Without breaking the kiss, he pushed it down to her waist. She began fumbling with the buttons of his shirt, her mind reeling. She had come a long way sexually, in a very short period of time, but she had seen nothing like the sheer debauchery that was going on all around her. She heard a voice telling her that this was all very wrong. It was easy to ignore.

Piers broke away. He tore off his jacket, unknotted his bow-tie and kicked off his shoes as he watched Kate step out of the dress and her shoes and pull down her tights.

'Perfect,' he said. He sat on the edge of the bed and pulled off his socks then stood up to strip off his trousers. His large erection was poking through the fly of his boxer shorts.

Kate stepped forward and gripped it in her hand, making a fist and squeezing it hard. She felt a surge of passion as she felt his cock throb convulsively. She dropped to her knees, releasing it temporarily, pulled the white boxer shorts down to his ankles, then seized his cock again. Pulling back his foreskin so sharply that he moaned, she slipped his phallus into her mouth and sucked on his glans. Then she pushed forward until his whole phallus was buried in her mouth and she could feel it butting into her throat. She ran her hand down to his scrotum and cupped his balls, jiggling them up and down in her fingers.

Her excitement was extreme. She closed her eyes. Burnt into her retina, as though she had looked into the direct sun, was the image of Sarah's naked body, plump and wholesome, her breasts swaying pendulously, her back forming a bridge between the two men at either end of her. She'd never seen her friend naked before, let alone having sex. She wondered what it would feel like to sink her hands into that pliant flesh and her clitoris pulsed against her labia.

She concentrated on Piers, bobbing her head back and forth, tonguing the underside of his cock, bathing it in her saliva, then swallowing it again as deep as it would go. She felt it throbbing.

'No,' he said, his voice husky and low-pitched. 'Not like that.'

He took her shoulders and pulled her to her feet, his cock pulled from her mouth. Kissing her on the lips again, he turned her round and pressed her back so they both sat on the edge of the bed. Then his hand came up to her breasts, moving across both of them, tweaking her nipples.

She allowed him to push her onto her back. He climbed onto the bed and knelt beside her, taking the waistband of her small black panties in his hands and pulling it down her long legs. When he got to her ankles, he tugged them clear, then picked up her left leg and began to kiss her calf. He worked all the way up to her knee, his eyes staring at her sex.

Kate wriggled her leg out of his clutches and moved over to the centre of the bed. Knowing that his eyes were still riveted to her sex, she splayed her legs. 'Watch me,' she said. The words excited her almost as much as they clearly did him; his cock twitched visibly.

Kate ran both hands down between her legs. She pulled the thick lips of her sex apart, letting him see the glistening wet interior, then pushed a finger up against her clitoris. It was already swollen. It pulsed as she touched it. She flattened it against her body then dragged it from side to side. Instantly she felt her nerves changing gear, readying themselves for what was now inevitable.

'I like to see that,' he said, his eyes transfixed. He took his cock in his hand and moved his fist gently up and down. Kate increased the speed of her gyrations, undulating her hips at the same time. She hadn't thought about any of this. From the moment her suspicions had been confirmed downstairs she had reacted instinctively, allowing her body to take control. She didn't want to have to think about what it all meant or have moral qualms. All that mattered was the way she felt. She didn't know why she wanted to let him see her come like this, but she did and badly.

'Yes,' she muttered, as her feelings mounted, becoming ever stronger, her orgasm building, the tell-tale signs making her nerves tingle.

She looked into Piers's eyes. He was a perfect stranger and she was behaving like a whore, all the old taboos abandoned – and that was what was exciting her, quite as much as the physical sensations. Being at this party, seeing what she had seen, was yet another milestone on the road to self-discovery.

She felt a surge of pleasure arc up from her clitoris. She arched her buttocks off the bed, aiming her sex at him and in that moment felt her sex convulse wildly as her orgasm exploded.

But almost before she had time to register it, he was on her. He literally threw his body on top of hers, his hands groping for her wrists, his thighs pressed together between her legs, his big cock forcing its way up inside her, her vagina a lake of liquid. In one thrust he had penetrated the whole length of her sex. Whether this lightning assault managed to extend and heighten the orgasm she had induced or create another new one, she did not know, but she knew she was feeling another violent surge of pleasure and she moaned loudly and panted for breath, her passion eating up all her oxygen.

Piers wrapped his arms around her tightly and rolled over onto his back, taking her with him. His cock sprang out of her but as she came to her knees, squatting on top of him, he thrust it back inside. With the regularity of a metronome he pounded into her, his body strong and quite as hard as his cock. It may have been minutes but it felt like hours as they lay together, wrapped around each other, sharing every sensation, Kate feeling his pleasure quite as much as she felt her own. She knew he was coming and knew she would come with him, too.

Though the length of her vagina clung to him tightly, a velvet glove sheathing his bone-hard flesh, at the neck of her womb Kate had the sensation that she was opening for him like a flower, letting him in, making a place for him to come. And it was that feeling, she knew, which finally set him off. She felt his thrusts slow and his body clench, his muscles becoming rigid one by one, until his whole body was like steel and he was completely still, his cock buried in the new place it had created, in the core of her. Then suddenly his cock began to jerk convulsively against the silky wet walls of her vagina and he ejaculated, jets of semen inundating her; she came too, pushing herself down on him with every ounce of energy, determined to wring every last drop of feeling from her body and his own.

And then the mood changed completely – as dramatically as if a switch had been thrown. The dark clouds rolled in; after the brightness of the sun, the storm began.

As Kate opened her eyes, she felt a weight shift on the bed. She glanced over her shoulder. A naked man was kneeling over her body. He had his erect penis in his hand and was oiling it with cream from a small tube. Throwing the tube aside, he pressed his cock down between Kate's buttocks.

'No,' she screamed. But the trouble was, she didn't mean no. She meant 'yes' and he knew it.

She felt her sphincter resist then give way. What she had imagined so graphically under the black silk blindfold in Gerard's house was actually happening. Her body shuddered as the man pressed himself into the depths of her anus. Piers was still erect enough for her to feel both phalluses nestling alongside each other, separated only by the thinnest of membranes.

'Oh, God . . .'

The man pulled back, then thrust forward again. By the time he had done this a second time the shock and the realisation of what was happening to her, quite as much as the surge of almost unbelievable physical sensations, took her instantly to the brink of coming again. But that was not what brought her off. As she found herself wriggling her buttocks back on the man, a man she told herself she had never even seen before, she felt a new sensation. Piers's cock was stirring. In seconds she felt it hardening and beginning to move inside her vagina. That was what caused a sharp, almost painful orgasm to course through her body, making her shudder, the feeling of being sandwiched between two bodies only adding to the symphony of unaccustomed sensations that assailed every part of her.

But that was still not the end. When she looked up again she saw the man who had been with

235

Patsy stepping up onto the bed. He was naked, with a rather small but very broad cock sticking out from underneath a large belly. Climbing onto the bed and kneeling astride Piers's head, he lifted her head and guided her mouth onto his erection. She took it deep into her mouth. Two cocks inside her, and now three.

'Now that is really something.' The voice came from a woman. Without being able to move her head, Kate swivelled her eyes round to see who it was. She could just glimpse Patsy standing by the side of the bed. She was unzipping the green dress; it fell to the floor. Under it she was wearing a pair of white hold-ups with narrow white welts and nothing else. Her breasts were small and pert and her pubis was completely hairless. Kate could see the slit at the top of her labia was as slick as her mons.

'My turn next, Piers, you promised me.'

She opened the top drawer of the bedside chest and took out a very large pink rubber dildo, crudely shaped to resemble an erect penis. Kneeling on the bed beside the four of them, she pushed the dildo up into her own sex. There was obviously little resistance.

Piers's cock was fully erect again now. Kate could feel it powering into her. The two men established a rhythm, one pushing forward as the other pulled out. But the one in her rear was coming. She felt his cock throb and swell, stretching her anus painfully. She moaned, the sound muffled on the third sword of flesh. As she felt the second cock jerking wildly inside her, the one in her mouth began to spasm too. Almost simultaneously the two men came, jetting their semen into her.

And still it wasn't over. As the two men pulled away, leaving Piers in sole occupation again, she felt Patsy moving down the bed. Free to move her head now, she watched as the redhead dipped her head down between her legs. She felt the softness of Patsy's mouth descending onto her thigh. It sucked on the base of Piers's cock, making it twitch convulsively. Piers moaned. Though he had only come moments before, his cock began to throb. Patsy sucked his balls into her mouth and ran her tongue over them.

The impact of Patsy's mouth was having an effect on Kate, too. The tiny voice at the back of her mind telling her that she shouldn't be enjoying any of this was getting louder but she could not ignore her physical reactions. She could feel Patsy's thigh rubbing against hers and her hot breath playing over her labia. She could also feel Piers's cock pulsing violently inside her. And then she came again, a wave of feeling rolling over her, wiping away everything, the centre of her universe reduced to her sex clenched reflexively around Piers's hard penis.

He must have come, too, because he yelped with pleasure; but Kate did not feel it. She felt nothing else. Nothing at all.

When she opened her eyes again she was lying on her back and Patsy was lying beside her. To her amazement, Sarah and Gerard were standing by the bed with Piers and the other two men. They were all naked.

'Go on,' Gerard said, nudging Sarah.

Kate could see that Sarah's eyes were on fire with excitement, little sparks of light dancing in her irises. Sarah climbed onto the bed. Without any hesitation she straddled Patsy's shoulders and pressed her sex down on her mouth. She leant forward, took hold of the pink rubber dildo that was still embedded in Patsy's vagina, pulled it out, then bent her head forward and kissed her hairless labia, grinding her mouth down on them. Both women moaned simultaneously, their bodies shuddering. Then they settled into a rhythm, chewing and licking at each others's sex, their mutual orgasms inevitable.

Kate felt nothing. Slowly she got up off the bed. The men were concentrating on the new spectacle and no one stopped her. She picked up her dress and stepped into it, found her shoes and panties and tights and carried them out into the corridor.

Through the open door opposite, she saw a large fat man lying on the obligatory double bed. One of the waitresses, still dressed in the white satin body, was sitting on his face, the crotch of the body pressed to his mouth, while another pretty and naked woman sat astride his hips. She was bouncing up and down on him like a rodeo rider, impaling his cock inside her.

Kate put on her shoes. She pulled the panties up her legs and zipped up the dress. She held the tights in her hand. She must have left her handbag downstairs, though she had no memory of doing so. As she walked down the corridor, she heard cries of ecstasy, moans of agony and gasps of pleasure from every side, but she ignored them, looking straight ahead. Nor did any of the sounds find any resonance in her body. It felt completely dead.

She walked downstairs and into the living room. Her handbag was on one of the chairs. The blonde in the black basque was lying on the floor on top of the woman in the short white dress. The dress was rucked up around the woman's waist and their mouths were pressed between their thighs while a man, a giant of a man with a huge head and massive plate-like hands, knelt behind the blonde, pulling her back onto his enormous erection.

Kate picked up her bag. Something snapped in her. Walking was no longer good enough; she broke into a run. She ran out into the vestibule and over to the front door. She threw the front door open and ran out into the gravel drive. She had no money and no means of getting home, but she didn't care. She just had to get away.

She began running down the drive. She tripped and fell, tearing the dress and her knee on the gravel. She jumped to her feet and began running again, but she had turned an ankle and the pain slowed her down. It was stupid, she knew. The road outside was only a country lane and she'd be putting herself in danger, trying to get a lift in the clothes she was wearing. But she was not listening to reason. She just had to get away.

She heard a car coming up behind her. She moved over to the grass verge. It drove a few yards ahead of her, then stopped. It was Gerard's Rolls.

'Hey, are you all right?'

The blond chauffeur climbed out of the car. He faced her, blocking her way.

'Please . . .' she said, trying to dodge to the left.

He moved to block her way so quickly that she ran into him. 'What's the matter?' he asked, his voice gentle and kind.

'Please, could you take me home? Please?'

He didn't say a word. He put his arm round her shoulders, guided her over to the car and opened the passenger door. She climbed inside, curled up on the rear seat in a foetal position and began to cry.

'There's brandy in the cocktail cabinet,' he said, as he got behind the wheel.

'Are you going to take me home?' she asked, fearful that he would turn her round and deliver her back to the house.

In answer, he accelerated. The big car surged forward. The wrought-iron gates opened automatically. An hour later she was home.

Chapter Eleven

SUNDAY MORNING. KATE woke late. She had slept badly, her sleep invaded by nightmares that were so close to the truth, so interwoven with the reality of what had happened to her, that she found it hard to distinguish between the two. She dreamt that she was back in the bedroom, with Piers and the others. At first it was just the same as it had been earlier, with Piers and the other man sandwiching her between them. But then she dreamt in graphic detail that it was her and not Patsy that Sarah had straddled. She seemed to be able to feel Sarah's plump flesh pressing down on her and her mouth sinking into her sex. Egged on by the others, Sarah's tongue explored the interior of her labia. The shock as it nudged against her clitoris had woken Kate up, her eyes wide, her clitoris pulsing as strongly as if the events were real.

Her body was sore. Whereas before this soreness had been welcome, worn as a badge of pride, now it was unpleasant. As she finally got out of bed and went into the bathroom to shower, every inch of her body felt battered and bruised. Apart from a real soreness around her sex, it was all in her imagination, she knew. The mirror revealed no marks on her body. The bruises were all in her mind.

She dried herself, put on her towelling robe and went down to the kitchen, feeling a real need for coffee. She picked the paper off the doormat. As the coffee machine bubbled, she sat at the kitchen table. It was another glorious morning, the strong sunlight highlighting the colours in her garden.

She felt too shattered to open the paper. She had gone too far: it was as simple as that. She had let her new-found enthusiasm run away with her, and it was all her own fault. Even if she hadn't known how the party would turn out – and, if she were honest with herself, she had known from the moment Gerard had invited her – she could have refused to take part. No one had forced her to do anything. She had no one to blame but herself.

As the coffee machine finished its cycle and she dragged herself to her feet, the door bell rang. She looked at her watch. It was twelve o'clock.

'Hi,' Sarah said brightly, as Kate opened the front door.

'God, you look sickingly energetic,' Kate said. 'Coffee's just brewed. Come in.'

They walked into the kitchen. Kate took out two mugs and poured coffee into both as Sarah sat down at the kitchen table.

'You look rough,' she said.

'Thank you. You certainly don't.'

Sarah was wearing a bright green sweatshirt and a bright yellow pair of track-suit bottoms. Her eyes sparkled with life.

Kate put the coffee down and sat opposite her friend.

'So what happened to you last night?' Sarah asked.

'I ran away. Literally.'

'Really?'

'Luckily Gerard's chauffeur gave me a lift.'

'He didn't say anything.'

'What time did you leave?'

'Late. Very late. Two, three – God, I had a good time. I don't think I've ever come so many times in my life.'

'Don't talk about it.'

'Why not? I thought it was all your idea.'

'I suppose it was. It was just . . . it just . . .' Kate suddenly felt herself on the edge of tears.

'Hey, it's all right.' Sarah stroked her friend's hand.

Kate pulled herself together. 'It all got too much for me. I think it's all happened too fast. I knew what I was doing at the beginning. I mean, I was really having a wonderful time. But that was just too much; I have to take it more slowly.' If at all, she thought, but did not say. The way she felt at the moment, she wasn't sure she ever wanted to have sex again. 'You, on the other hand,' she said, 'looked as though you were having a ball.'

'Too right. Gerard was all over me. He's invited me to his house for lunch. I came over to pick up my car.' Sarah's Mercedes was still parked outside. 'And . . .' she hesitated.

'And what?'

'Gerard wondered if you'd like to come, too?'

Kate laughed. 'He never gives up, does he? What's he hoping for – a command performance, the two of us together?'

'Something like that.'

Kate caught an expression in her friend's eye that suggested Gerard wasn't the only one who hoped that might happen. 'Sorry, Sarah.'

'Oh well, I told him I'd ask. I'd better go. I'm late already.'

'Have fun.'

'Thanks for inviting me to the party, in the first place,' she said, getting to her feet, most of her coffee undrunk. 'I'll call you tomorrow, let you know how I got on.'

At the front door, Sarah took her friend by the shoulders and kissed her cheek. As Kate was about to move away, Sarah held her firmly for a moment and brushed her lips against Kate's mouth. Then she grinned like a schoolgirl who'd been caught smoking cigarettes behind the bushes.

'Any time, Kate,' she said, waved and ran to her car.

Kate could imagine what awaited her at Gerard's: the strange room, and the metal cabinet. She wondered if the blond chauffeur would be on duty again, ready to do his master's bidding.

With a feeling of determination, Kate went back upstairs. She collected the white plastic waste-bin she kept in the bathroom and took the dildo out of the top drawer of her bedside chest, dropping it into the bin. She added all the letters she kept from her advertisement in 'Kindred Spirits'. She didn't want any of the numbers. She didn't want to call Pamela or Peter or Marianne. She didn't want to talk to Tom. They were all tarred with the same brush, all celebrants of a ritual that had lost its meaning for her.

She had no idea what she was going to do now. She had her senior partnership and her professional success. The promotion would mean more money. She could think about a new house. She'd have to choose a new car.

She felt a wave of tiredness overtake her. She lay on the bed and closed her eyes. In the darkness, images waited to ambush her, sudden vivid presentations of Piers's naked body and of Sarah's. Her sex throbbed, the soreness of it only increasing the tingling sensations it produced.

She sat up, annoyed with herself for dwelling on it. All that was over for her, now, and she had to accept it. She got to her feet again and picked up the waste-bin. Some more letters had arrived from the *City Times* on Saturday morning. She had been too busy thinking about the party to open them. They could go in the bin too.

The letters were stuffed at the side of the toaster on the white kitchen work-surface with all the household bills. She took them out. There were four. She threw them into the waste-bin, then renewed the coffee in her mug.

She stared at the unopened letters sitting in the bin. She took one out, a white envelope addressed in neat capitals, then threw it back in the bin again, then took it out again and tore the envelope open. A photograph fell out. It was of a man in his thirties with thick brown hair. He was dressed in a crisp blue shirt and navy slacks.

Kate opened his letter with no intention of reading it. She scrunched it up, threw it into the bin. Almost immediately, she took it out again and flattened the paper out.

Dear Box 43,
Like you, I want a lover. I want to make love. I'm enclosing a photograph. I have a good sense of humour and fun and I know what I want. From the tone of your ad I think you're probably exactly the same. That's the point, isn't it? Sex is about knowing what you want and going out to get it. I'm not indiscriminate. If you're interested, then let's meet for a drink and talk. Just talk. Who knows what talking can lead to?
James

Kate balled the letter up and threw it into the bin again, then took it out to the dustbins at the back of the house. The warmth of the sun made her feel better. She was hungry, too, she realised, which she thought was a good sign.

She liked the tone of James's letter. She liked his attitude. He was right. It was what she'd felt over the past weeks, knowing what she wanted and

246

going out to get it. But all that was over now.

Back in the kitchen she opened the fridge. There was some lettuce and tomatoes and a pack of prosciutto, but nothing else. She could drive to the supermarket and buy some food, or she could go to the local Italian. No, she didn't want to eat alone.

She looked at the kitchen table and cursed herself. She'd forgotten to throw the photograph of James away. She picked it up. His telephone number was scrawled on the back. Oddly it was the same exchange as hers. He must live close by.

She didn't want to eat alone, and she was hungry. It wouldn't do any harm to call him and ask if he'd like to come out to lunch, would it? She didn't have to go to bed with him; her commitment to a new and heavily sensible life wouldn't be altered by that.

She picked up the phone and dialled his number.

A hour later she was sitting in La Genoa. She was wearing a summer dress over her white La Perla teddy and flesh-coloured hold-up stockings. She told herself these were more comfortable than tights and cooler. She decided she was never going to wear tights again in the summer. Her choice of lingerie was entirely governed by practical considerations, she told herself. And she almost believed it.

He was five minutes late. She saw him come in. He raised his hand. He was wearing a light blue shirt, open at the neck, and beige-coloured trousers. His face was tanned. He had large, slightly hooded blue eyes, a jutting firm chin and bushy eyebrows.

He walked towards her table. 'Hello,' he said, 'I'm James.'

'I'm Kate.'

She had made the right decision, she thought. She hated eating alone. They would talk and she could gaze into his eyes and wonder what it would be like to press herself against his slender body, and kiss his rather small mouth, and hold his growing erection in her hand. Not that she had any intention of doing that, of course. She was committed. Sex was pushed onto the back burner again. She had taken one step too far. She wasn't going to make that mistake again. Definitely not. She wasn't going to let him seduce her. She wasn't going to seduce him.

Well, not until after lunch, at least.

Other bestselling X Libris titles available by mail: